MORE THAN 100 PAGES

Aleen Bharati

BookSquirrel Publication®

BookSquirrel Publication®

Mahadev Totala Nager, Indore (M.P), 452001
Regd Under MSME
Website: *www.booksquirrelpublication.com*

"More Than 100 Pages"

By: Aleen Bharati

ISBN: 978-81-946524-7-2

English Self Help 1ts Edition

Book Editing: Priya Pradhan

Cover Design: Aleen Bharati(Author)

DEDICATION

I want to dedicate this book to the teenagers, college students, and people who are at their early working age.

Being young, I believe we are the ones ready for the future.

ABOUT THE AUTHOR

"Every Life has the same concept, only the pattern changes"

"Sometimes it is special to be called crazy"

– Aleen Bharati

Aleen Bharati was born on 25th October, 2000. He was born in Patna, Bihar and brought up in Panchgram (Hailakandi), Assam.

He is known for his unique Identity and get a name as "Author Alien." He is known for his Travel Experience with his Live-Sketching skills on the roads, Story Telling, Contemporary and Abstract Art forms, Poetries, etc.

Being close to nature, he devoted his heart, mind and soul to the epiphany of nature. Being a nature-lover he has always observed multiple sides of nature.

Design, creativity and technological approach have been his true fascination, and therefore, he is pursuing Bachelors in Architecture from Mumbai, Maharashtra(2019-2024).

Being creative and /driven by words, he set on a venture having been enhanced in his writing abilities - books like "Alone Alive", and "Dolorous" are international publications in which he contributed his content. He has also been the co-author in 20+ anthologies among which some are even registered for Indian and World Book of Records.

Apart from his Architectural studies, he admires photography and an artistic lifestyle.

He is a true enthusiast who loves to grab wisdom and prudence from confidence, self-belief, rationality and experience.

Email – aleen.bharati0625@gmail.com

Instagram - @aleen.official_ / Aleen Bharati

An Ethereal Observation by a 19-year-old kid
(When he published this book- 1st edition)

NOTE FROM THE AUTHOR

"Don't say you are bad, only say you are good, but be better"

-Swami Vivekananda

You might have heard of those people, who experience problems in their life, but they still don't know what happens with them. And, even those people who are part of the same society, think, they don't have any experience. Many of us know the difference between real-life and virtual life, but how it puts an impact on us, we don't know.

This book is for those people who belong to this society but they are not aware of their own surroundings. They travel, they feel, they know, they experience, but what they lack is that they don't remember it. They are hurt, but even then they remain unaware of a few things.

So, as you read this, I am not going to say this is particularly for you or meant only for you, because experiences can teach any age group of people. On the whole, this book is focused on the people belonging to the 15-35years age group. However,

reading a piece of writing does not allow such limitation.
Read it, learn from it and extract your own conclusions out of it.

Love Leave WoRK SouNd play YOu Happy
Think WoRds Travel PeOple **ART** **House** CAre

Can you see the distorted words on the two lines above. Maybe that create a question is it a typing error, No its not.
Here we can see Distorted and disturbed things grabs our attention easily and we questions on that.
So don't get limited to this book's perspective. There are some outside for which you need to explore and yes that will be found distorted but it doesn't mean it has no value.

What kind of a book is this?

This book is intended to fill up the gaps in your experiences. You might have gone through them. You might feel something, or some experiences might have been your own. Well, this book will help you in the best way, in all the above conditions. You can learn things from the plots, you can gain knowledge, or you can relate your own situations with those in this book. It is not a novel but a book of experiences, which have been recollected by me. Don't stop reading. If you have some learnings, evaluate them and confirm them through the conclusions that reach you. If you love to explore things, read this book, and you'll see that your curiosity level definitely increases on its own. Underline the thoughts and emotions that you had experienced, or highlight an idea, if you learn something new from it.

GOOD LUCK

ACKNOWLEDGEMENT

I feel a little hesitant to write the Acknowledgement section, for whom to name and who to omit is difficult to decide. But I want to thank my parents, especially my mother, whose efforts make my roots strong.

This book would have been worthless without the support of my friends and those who always stood by me when I thought I was alone.

I express my gratitude to all my friends, who connected with me as strangers but I consider their cooperation to be highly valued, as now they have grown very close.

CONTENT

GENERAL STORIES

1. PHOTOGRAPHS, STORIES AND IF HE ASKS FOR...
2. THINGS THAT NEVER CHANGE (MONEY, YOU AND TIME)
3. THE LOVE NO ONE TALKS ABOUT
4. ONE DAY LATE; TRUCK DRIVER
5. WHEN IT'S ABOUT GIRLS

POETRY SECTION

1. THE PHOTO ALBUM
2. MY FESTIVE CALENDER
3. THE MAIL BOX
4. YES, I LOVE YOU
5. I HAVE KNOTS
6. I HAVE GLASSES, AM I LUCKY?
7. A PAIR OF SHOES
8. THE NAME

LEARN FROM EXPERIENCES

THE STORIES IN THE NAME OF TRUTH

From the next page you are going to relate your situation with it, maybe it had happened to you, maybe not, but you need to know them

The stories you are going to read are all written with the best possible combination of imagination and true experiences. Containing experiences that have left an imprint, the stories offer distinct clarity of the author's life, goals and values... They are generally based on reality, comprising both good and bad experiences.

All experiences are dipped into the ocean of tales which are written just to help you in your life. They will definitely assist you in fighting against the shambolic odds of the world. All the facts, figures and names mentioned are somehow not the exact ones but they are meaningfully outlined in the plot just to maintain the fluency of the thoughts reflected in the story.

Make sure you enjoy them, and if you need to learn anything, or if you extract a specific truth from any of the plots, use these stories as a workbook and mark a few lines to take a closer view of them.

The author, eventually, has tried to narrate these stories, reflecting that everyone experiences such things as can make one perplexed. A reader would like to tell them in the form of his story; another one would create his own story and yet another one would not even share it. So, being an individual, you can relate to one of the above categories, you may come out of a shadow to share your experiences with someone and convey your own truth. You will jot down in this process, the ramifications of the good and the bad that you might face, and the feelings you might relate to.

WEAK

WOOD

While venturing out into the woods, a 12-year-old girl Tayba was looking for logs to make fire so that the food could be prepared. Her father asked her to take the thin ones, which were generally eaten by termites. They collected two types of wood, the broken ones or rather, the eaten or weak ones. And, the other type: very strong, which had been chopped down by her father. Her father was a carpenter and wanted his daughter to get the best knowledge of the quality of the wood and its types. One night, they were sitting on a chair, when all of a sudden the chair broke. Luckily, her father was not hurt. Tayba helped him stand up and checked whether he was fine. He said, "I am graced that this wood is strong enough to hold my weight. Yes, you may have seen me sitting on a 4-legged chair, but deep down I was aware that I was sitting on a 3-legged chair, the fourth leg being the weak wood one. This 'weak wood' can be any one of us. Perhaps someone in the family, a worker in an office, or a member of a team."

Often, we hear that if you want to break a log of wood, you can easily do it, but if you want to break a bundle of woods, chances are that you will fail. Did you understand the statement? Very easy, right? It is teamwork and unity. We've often heard that unity is strength. Yes, it is, but you are born as an individual. Right? So, are you aware of these individuals? The man who earns and buys you a pen is your father and the woman cooking food for you at home is your mother or vice versa. Maybe both do the two sets of activities in their turn. The main question is, do you really have their hands on your head as your safest shield? If you are born as an individual, you have to accept that one day you have to live your life independently. For this reason, Tayba's father thought to have a talk with his daughter.

In the words of her father, "If our whole body is a chair, and if we break our leg, we can still stand but the only condition required is balance. Substitution is another reason to stand but unless you have the right balance, you will lose respect or you might be thrown out like stinking garbage."

, He continued, "You know, Tayba, that you can be considered worthless!"

Hurt at his words, Tayba protested. "How could I be considered worthless? I cut the wood and help my parents in their work, caring less about my physical health."

Her father smiled and said, “You can be considered worthless because you don’t know your own worth! Do you know who you are? What all can you do?”

Indeed, if she was not in her true ‘self’ she would just be used by others, perhaps even her parents, what to say of anyone else. The truth from which we couldn’t run away was that it was a chair and it could only be used for sitting. In this context, we can say that the chair is used just for sitting but not for decoration and cannot be used as a table. According to her father, the concept was inadequate, because he did not question about its specialty, i.e., the chair can only be used for sitting. Through his words, he conveyed that the chair would be used only for sitting until and unless it was redesigned to be used for other purposes.

Referring to the incident he said,, she had tried something different from the usual thing, which was not about the beauty - he talked about the productiveness for her. A piece of wood could be used to make a chair and a bed, too, and that would increase its worth. An individual is always born first, he works to be in the first place, works in the first place, experiences things in the first place and even when he or she is dead, he will remain in the first place.

"While you grow, don't work only for me," her father said.. Then her father took her to the riverside and placed the chair on the sand.

He said, "Tayba, my child, the chair is useless but one can still use it when there is no place to sit." He sat on that chair, the three-legged one, and showed her that by applying the concept of balance and innovation, he put to good use something useless - something that most people would have discarded.

Inspiring her thoughts, he asked her that if she went into the forest, what would she generally look for - only woods or a different variety of woods? Her reply was nonchalant, "I would look for diverse wood types." To which he said, "I have never asked you just to look for a specific type of wood or even different types of woods." He further added, "When I enter into the forest, I think about something new that we can rebuild or recreate. Sometimes, we take a few things which have no use at the given moment, but it can be put to use later - say, at the time of flood to build the refugee centers or something else to prevent the flood damage."

Planning is a quality and it should be nourished every time. Sometimes luck may not support you, just like it happened with Tayba's father. In the rainy season, he didn't get proper wood, only the wet ones here and there. The spark of exploration and patience ought to be present inside everyone. So, he concluded with an amazing idea. 'Parents love you because you are their flesh and blood. However, they can only provide you with the basic articles of need during your childhood. Ensuring real growth and development is possible by your own exploration.. What can you do other than using your capability and specialty? In other words, do you want to be a chair or anything else? Or, would you just change your looks? Or, do you want to be known only for one thing, or for a few other things? Don't allow someone to use you only as a chair - yes in the first phase of your socialization,, you will be treated in a similar way.. But keep on exploring and making yourself productive. Try to do something different. Start from being a simple chair and become a chair of high worth with more than one value or usage.

Having discussed all of these, Tayba's father asked her, "Tell me, did you learn something different from me today?"

Tayba replied, "I did!"

What she understood was how to learn different perspectives from the same incidents and ideas. A broken chair could teach her about the weakness in human character coming out under pressure. The importance of redesigning oneself and knowing one's own worth was impressed upon her by seeing how just one broken leg could put a good chair out of use. Thrusting that same 3-legged chair in the sand showed her how important innovation and balance were. The fact that the broken chair could be put to use as a protective barrier against flood damage taught her that nothing could be deemed useless, as circumstances could change one's worth. So much, from just a weak piece of wood!

THE HALLOW OF FACEBOOK

Have you ever made a Facebook account? Did you ever put information about yourself on your profile? From a small point to an entire line, I mean to say, even the most basic details you add, like: your name, address, date of birth, mobile number, you even add the names of the members of your family. You might have experienced inhibition when Mark Zuckerberg asked you to fill a few spaces before starting your daily routine. Yes, Facebook has become a part of everyone's daily routine.

But now tell me, was your account ever hacked? Did someone ever steal your information? Someone texted you many times and you blocked him or her. Generally, we consider it as 'HIM.' Because girls never go for all this, do they? I know most people will agree with me. But, no, you are wrong. Let's switch on our torches and start hunting for the truth!

It was 2014 and he was thinking about an activity outside his business. The glass boy, yes, he had got this name from his friends. Why? Just because he wore glasses! Not cool ones, rather simple ones, but unlike Harry Potter's. For he looked cool behind them and his character suited his glasses. Moving further ahead with this plot, he had a mobile. Lamentably, he didn't have any knowledge about creating a Facebook account. He took the help of his friend who guided him about its basics. Understanding Facebook was difficult at first, but he tried with sincerity and concentration. His friend was also a kind person who patiently answered all his questions. Within a few days of getting the basic knowledge, he was taught by him how to fill his school's name, his date of birth, and if he wanted to add, he could add his nickname, too. What next? His friend gave him his account and suggested him to change the password, which he did. The glass boy changed his password and even sent requests to many of his friends on the social platform. He was content with his record, but Facebook needed internet, for which he asked help from his parents - an amount equal to about 1 dollar.

He managed to use Facebook to chat with others, and then he mastered the use of the platform with his circle of friends. And, after a few days, he was getting friend requests from others, too. He started receiving friend requests from people he knew and from even from those he didn't know. One night, late at 1 pm, he looked for

somebody he knew. As numerous profiles were thrown up on the search page, he tried to make sense with a precise name. He figured out something which was new to him; momentarily, his 'friend-list' increased to 50 and he sent requests to 20 more.

He continued updating his profile. However, that page consistently showed the message that "you are 70% done." As a matter of first importance, Facebook never allows members below 18 to open an account. However, like many others, he made a record through the assistance of his friend by deceiving the software. He set his introduction to the platform five years back. These stages are made for social connections; however, they have limitations.

As far as the terms and conditions are concerned, they are irrelevant for those under 18, because you are not mature enough for this. But we are one of those who love to break rules, right? And it results in illegal entrance. How many of our parents know about us? A few know but most have no idea regarding this, for two reasons - lack of knowledge about the platform or indifference to an unknown field? The platform was being used by an under-aged teenager. Suddenly, he explored a page that had links to various female profiles. How everyone acts on a platform? No one knows, yes, it's true, only Facebook knows what you are up to? His friend list started increasing with a three-digit-number. Now, he learned more about how to interact with new friends.

He had skills: writing poems, lines, even doing artwork, and he shared them on Facebook. But once again he was at a loss, annoyed with that line, "Your profile is 72% complete." He was not working anywhere, but like other similar profiles he set the text "I am a student" and later he changed it to "Working at student." Again, a back door was selected. Now giving more light to it, for a clearer vision, he used Facebook with a browser, "www.facebook.com" instead of using the Facebook application. When, he was up to these activities, the cell phones generally came with a button system and were available in different types.

Growing up in the era of digital platforms, devices are being upgraded with a new mind system. One such came with a Facebook application added inside, and they called it handshakes in the business. So unlike others, he was happy with his handset. But one day, one main button of his handset began to malfunction. The clear button got damaged. .Given his situation, he had the only option to keep using it, and he needed to get acclimated to it. A few days and weeks, therefore, he struggled with typing sentences with correct spellings. But, after a long practice, he dealt with it. In fact, he even typed four to six lines of seven words each without a single mistake, and at good speed. He could type two lines within five to ten seconds. He was now getting friend requests even from foreign countries. He texted desperately to many, and even got blocked by many. Then, he realized that if he had to develop well he should appear to be reliable and he accepted, he had to improve his English language skills for better global communication. The speed at which he learnt English from games and this social platform was 20% to 30%, higher than s his school room learning.

He developed the quality of patience against ignorance and rejection. Through his profile, a few more people joined him, being members of the same Facebook groups. Still, it didn't satisfy him. He made a habit of updating his profile with an aim to grab the attention of new people. Several times he made some changes in his profile with the basic options, like his name, choosing nicknames with an English feel. Then he changed "working at student" to "not yet working", as he was looking for a professional tag. Then, he switched to his nickname and started adding other information about him. Yes, now he was getting new friends, but still all his "friend-requests" were not getting accepted by several. The acceptance-rate had increased by 30 to 40%. People were now interacting with him. He was getting better known by his virtual name which soon became his virtual identity, and the permanent one. He shared his real identity with a few people and with those who later became the closest friends. The circle he had in his real life still didn't stop teasing him with his old name, but, as he was used to bullying or teasing, he simply ignored them. Gradually, a time came when no one had queries about his virtual activities. Once in a while, a few people did come up with questions with respect to which he politely indicated the referred word, which was his chosen nickname, and explained its importance and suitability.

But did someone find anything strange? No one cared in the least. He had made his fake identity inside that platform just for attention and interaction. Many individuals just liked him, relished a space where they were treated as normal, respected and also made true friends. He might not be doing something awful, but making a virtual and fake identity was bound to create a problem for him sometime or the other. And, not to forget, while had his virtual world with a number of so-called virtual friends, they were all real, as a matter of fact. A few faked themselves but there were also the original ones, whom he was cheating. Among all these, he had his girlfriend, and the time came when two individuals began to connect themselves with emotions. His girlfriend was from Indonesia, and as new to the Facebook platform as he was.

Let's skip the fake side, and think about their true emotions. Yes, they loved each other virtually, but they had respect for each other and even shared their experiences once a day or once a week. They spent their real time in the virtual world. They helped each other solve real problems - like science and math - on the virtual platform!

No matter, but surely it broke when the time came to reveal the truth. She told him that she already had a boyfriend. She added that she loved him, too, but he was far from her. There were thousands and lakhs of kilometers between them. He felt hurt when he found that he had been treated as a toy. He thought what she would feel when she would know that the person she

was engaging with was a guy already bullied and troubled by the people around him and had no proper image in real life?
This changed him, yes. But the real tough time came when his account was hacked 10 times, within two years. Just because of his access to new people and the chats he had with his friends. He was upset, even shocked, for a few days and he wondered how he could get his account back. In the early days, a few of his real-life friends had helped him, but now, he had to learn how to hack Facebook accounts because no one outside the country was hacking his account. It was the people surrounding him who wanted to play with him and tease him. "So, new ways lead to new doors."

He learnt to hack accounts and figured out that a few people cheated him. Hence, he decided to create a fake account. This time too, he didn't have any intent to hurt anyone, but this time, he planned to keep an eye on people around him and ascertain what they were up to.

What happens when an individual gets disturbed? When he becomes a source of problem for others? These were two questions that could never be resolved because of the fact that they were fully dependent on the situation of that person and of the prevalent conditions. Days and years went off. After a long and deep research, he extracted various issues and many problems. He found that there were many individuals who had one real face but he or she had more than one account on the Facebook platform. A few profiles or names were in demand, but only for trolling, a few were busy demoralizing someone or cheating on someone, and a few were blocked while many were newly created. But what he figured out after all this was rather amazing. Let's see what he concluded.

He spent more than four years with Facebook and got to know it well. The people who were operating on that platform consisted of three categories. The first category obviously consisted of the real ones, who generally got connected to it because they didn't have access to any other platforms. There were some who had mastered it while the others didn't want to switch to other platforms. In addition, there were some who had joined because of the games connected to their Facebook accounts. Then, the second category was the page owners or the business owners who were using Facebook for business handshakes. The third category was of people who needed to be cool, and longed to be connected to people - they needed to become the part of a large crowd. They didn't bother about lacking knowledge about how to run their account securely and safely. But, they used it for some political ends or to brainwash the gullible ones on various topics. It sounded genuine for the platform was formulated to connect users across the globe. The most important group of individuals - and I hope you understood who I am referring to - gathered all one's basic details from there for misusing. Facebook is still working on its security, but the way it grew, it does show a dark future. The deep truth was that it was all about business, whether with you or with others, and no matter it was with your details. Now in addition to this, Facebook gave and is still giving space to, many people on its platform, to answer irrational questions and, though it may initially appear funny, the information can be used by others later on.

Other sites take one's information and create problems for one. This was the loophole he found in Facebook.

We need to understand, if Facebook is not wrong then this is also true that it is not fully correct. Don't boycott Facebook, it needs to be present there to connect with new people, but do understand with whom you are interacting. Look for the information about you that you have made available online. Don't give your precise details, ever. New people cannot be your close and loyal ones, and they can even use your location to trap or harass you. Not just the future, even the present is not safe. I was the glass boy that day, even now I wear glasses but the simple and plain ones that help me see clearly.

RETURNING FROM THE BLIND HEAVEN

It was a late evening, and someone pulled me up from a second height where I had reached by rolling down the highest level of the mountain. I was just four steps away from the road to the hidden depth of the chasm of the mountains. Yes, that was my third time.

"A week ago, I was sitting on a branch near a tree, and was engaged in playing my mouth organ. It's hard to learn without regular practice, but whenever I felt alone, I played that instrument, no matter how horribly I played. Hello there, I am Stalwart, you are just inside the pages of this book, and watching me do what I was doing. By watching I mean imagining, and if you are not imagining then you need to do so, for then, you can get to the depth of this story.

I am neither too old nor too young. Yes, you guessed it right, I am slightly older than a teenager. If you are reading this story, then it's probably come out in a book form. Yes, now you may wonder a bit more about whether I am writing a diary. No! I tried many times to write, but the truth was so harsh that even I couldn't face it.. So, I burnt all that I had written. I know you have your own views and thoughts regarding death, heaven, peace, etc., but at the same time, you forget to think about life, breathing, movements, energy and so on. Now I am going to share my past life, and this is the 11th or the 12th time that I am doing this. Only this time, it may be taking the form of a piece of paper. It may be the last that I will be attempting to write.

The paragraph you just read was taken from a piece of paper which was found in a table's drawer while cleaning. I thought that day I was again a little depressed. And I had that mouth organ with me, not the older one, but a piece that looked similar to it, a chromatic mouth organ. I used to play it whenever I felt I was useless or that I was just an object for teasing by the bullies around me. It may be I was an example of the weakest person or the poorest boy. It was all about the truth of being alone, not physically, but mentally. I remembered the days when I was a little kid. I had taken a knife and stood in front of the mirror, taking the sharp edge near my neck. Was it terrifying? Yes, I know, for I had stopped because of fear.

Why this negative instinct came into my mind? No one had ever taught me that. Neither had I found that which ate me from inside.

The hilarious part of all of this was that I had the reputation of being the most talkative and the craziest kid that time. That time,

I had never discussed with my parents about the issues going on in my mind. I slept off with tears, and lied to them that I had been sweating the night before. And such lies worked for me for eight years from that day. As I grew, I found creativity in myself. But even that did not stop time from making me one of the weakest kids around. I ran, I laughed, I shouted, I spoke, even more, but every night was spent in silence, not the silence of sleep, it was the silence of gloom, when I thought only about the tough minutes or hours I'd spent in the day. My parents helped me a lot - as much as they could, but a "statement" ate me up from inside, a statement that I don't have the strength to speak. A day came, when my parents were not at home, so I stood in front of the mirror. That time, I realized I didn't have the strength to stand in front of my own eyes. Still, I asked myself why I was weak. Why I was ignored? Why everybody teased only me? Why some particular task could not be completed by me, the task that could be done by each and every one in the class? Why didn't I have the power to fight back? Why was I a failure? Why no one liked me? Why he could do it but I couldn't?

How could I believe in the normalcy of all this....? Like many of us, I had heard many a time that these situations are normal. But why do we need to skip that, I think skipping that makes our minds heavier. And it takes us to an unnamed place, where we can enter but there is no exit. I tried, spirituality, to make my mind calm. My mind processed many things at the same time, sometimes it made me cry. . Yes, a boy cried, a weak boy cried. And if someone knew it'd become headlines among people that I cried like girls. I think girls cry because they know how to control emotions, and how crying is important for draining out the inner problems tormenting hearts.

It is not easy for everyone to process everything in a simple way. Sometimes, teasing increased to such an extent that it became bullying. Yes, if I cry then I am weak, but then they will laugh. If I complain, then two conditions could follow: one, if the teacher took actions I was going to be bullied further because I was weak, couldn't be strong. In the second condition, the teacher would ignore all of this with a statement, that it's normal, and advise me to just smile through it. Which would mean I'd continue to get bullied as usual.

That was the society I was a part of, and so I kept myself silent for 8 years. And it resulted in my big step, my first **Suicide Attempt**.

I honestly tell you that I don't have the strength to write about it, which is why I am writing, not speaking about it. I tried many times to write in my diary that my family members found me weak just because I couldn't do normal calculations, I could not write answers properly and didn't understand anything in the first attempt. Both in my close circles and in the society outside, I found myself to be useless and that started creating gaps in my heart. Someone chose someone first who had already proven themselves for any work, he had value. But why I didn't even get a chance to prove, a chance to show and chance to be respected as valuable?

People may think that a kid, a boy or a girl, cannot be harmed too badly by anything. The point is, how many people have you deeply interacted with who understand if they have really something to share? Such people are never going to share, until they grow closer to you, consider you to be a person with whom they can share their innermost secrets. The insecurity of being alone and the insecurity of being bullied is the most common sign of all kinds of depression. Society tells parents are the main reason for everything, but it is not only they, even you are responsible for his or her situation. Sometimes a friend can help more than a parent can.

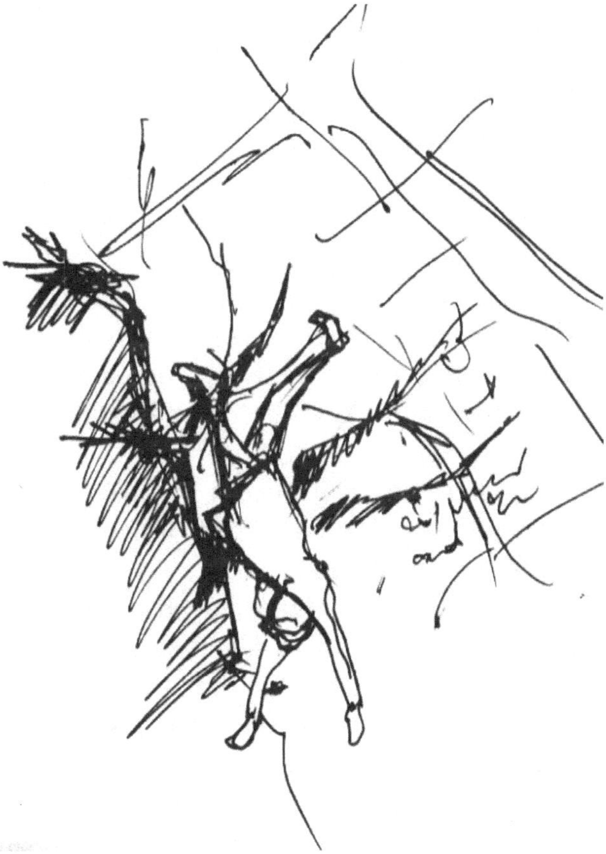

I don't know how many nights I cried; a few rare days were the worst, when I would get shocked by the intensity of my grief while crying and went senseless.
The day came when I was going somewhere with my friends, walking down the middle of the road. I told my friends that I was not able to came, though I had lied to them and even to my parents. That day I had the bigger fear enveloping me, what type of life I would get after death and how people would treat my parents. Yes, they would cry, I felt sure they would cry a lot, but after a few days everything would go back to its normal state.

I was at the edge of a road, a quiet, dark place with no streetlights and where rarely anyone came. I asked for forgiveness, in the air, and I cried as I jumped.
After about 10 to 15 minutes, I was found hanging from a tree and some bushes, about 4 steps away from a monstrous hole.. I was faced with two choices now, going ahead, or going back. I chose the second option. As I climbed up and turned back, I realized I was doing what only a coward would do. Running away from problems. But the truth was that depression was something which could lead to any negativity. I went back home and I lied again, that I had fallen down the stairs. I got the necessary first aid and I was fine.
But many things were still revolving in my mind. I kept coming back to the thought that we were so much like jokers: we hide our sad faces to make others smile.
After that day, many things changed. I mean I changed them. That day, when I jumped, I got the meaning of strength, that if I had it for death or to face the blind heaven then I could have built it to live a better and stronger life on earth and to have an honorable self- image . Hard times never stopped in my path of life, and there were more to come, but what I could learn from this failed suicide attempt was that if I would not put my step

ahead and increase my strength , no one could help me do it. I changed myself, I earned many things just to create my image and I went a long way in the construction of an impressive self-image. Still I didn't share things with any of my friends. I mean the closest ones. It is only now that I have started it. I hope you would be holding my hand and would not laugh when I cry in front of you. We, the depressed people, we are not weak, we just need your support, true care and true love.

NEGLIGENCE AND PHOTOGRAPHY

What is your exact phase, when you get to know that you are one of the people who need true friends or a group like others have? It has always been easy to say that I am happy alone, and I don't need anyone. Mostly introverts have such thinking, as most of the people say. But the truth is far different from our thoughts. **Likewise**, truth and experience say, "The loneliness is directly dependent on the situation, the circumstances." So, the question again rises - who is alone? The answer is, you. What are the conditions that one has to undergo when one is in the state of solitude? Is there anything which overcomes it? If there is a question, then it is possible that there will be an answer, too. Go ahead with the story to find out.

The story begins with a boy, who was generally ignored by the technologically updated society for his lack of knowledge in the field of technology or device. People ignored, or it seemed, they weren't directly focused on talking to him. There was nothing that could change his daily life much, because he was a school student. And if you are in a school, it's a rare chance that you will be alone. The question still stood starkly: why did he feel lonely or for what reason was he ignored? **Rigid truths always shaped by struggling times**. Kumar, he was one of the guys who did his work creatively and carefully just to shine among others. Still, he was teased, because he didn't have knowledge.

There is a quote written by someone with a profound philosophical approach. He said,

"If you win anything, then you need someone to express your joy in front of him or her. But if you're alone in a field, then to whom will you express your feelings? In other words, people surrounding you matter."

Skip the thought of this internet life. Now-a-days many of us are inside this virtual world, with profiles, pages, faces, photos, biographies and many other things, found only in this un-real life. Let's hold a second and think about it: after everything that we have in real life, why do we need this virtual life? Did you ever ask yourself? I know, your answer will be no, because as the world is going ahead, we are with that until and unless we are not trapped inside the virtual life. Take a look at your surroundings: Do you feel any energy when you think this- "If you need someone, there will be someone who will take care of you?"

Kumar, he was one of the guys who talked to himself when he wanted someone to listen to him, but he didn't find anyone. I hope you will agree with him, because talking to ourselves helps distract us from our problems. But with that habit, which folks call craziness - yes, a person may be one, if he thinks others think so, too -he was addressed as the same, the crazy guy in front of any group. But he needed respect. Why it's always a problem of owning respect? It is always to be earned, right? Yes, it is. But have you ever learned how to earn respect? Yes, it's obvious that your parents helped you out in this. In addition, you keep on learning from time and experience. Now let's talk about a situation wherein we are alone, without a social life, and we get no respect or value in a group.

Kumar had accepted his fate of always getting teased by his mates. So, he decided to learn something from his parents. He started showing interest in many things. However, the habit of teasing was too old a way for people to give up. They carried it for their entertainment, and as a result they continued. A few helped in his interest but they taught him only what they thought he needed.

As a result, Kumar lost hope, even though his interest and likes were as before. He loved nature, and natural beauty was where his eyes got attracted to. What he could perceive, was never seen by others. He noticed that people loved seeing rare and extraordinary things, which caught people's eyeballs. Yes, he didn't have any high-rated accessories of good qualities. But, what he noticed in his surroundings was saved in his mind. He tried to capture moments of nature, and showed them to people like his parents, friends, and even people of his groups.

Unfortunately, he was still teased because of low quality work. They couldn't even compliment that they had seen a few unique things he had captured in his images! But at least they began to ask when he had seen that image and how he had captured them. How he got the shot? And many more questions. For the first time, he owned a smile on his face. Was it a change? He began to capture many moments and started displaying them. He had interest in art work; moreover, he possessed the skill of sketching and abstract art that also helped him nourish his photography skills and imagination or work. Then, as technology kept improving with time, his equipment became better as well. People loved to capture their moments so he asked their friend if he could take their pictures. Although they never took him anywhere with them, this time, they allowed. Now people talked about him, even in groups, and now he was known for his photography skills.

He never knew that he would be known for his work, because he had lost his respect and identity by his name. **It is valid on the off chance that you are not solid in something, but there are numerous things to learn and through that make a name after learning different aptitudes**. Now Kumar searched for virtual groups where pictures were shared. For example, take Facebook. Anybody who posted a group photo did not have Kumar with them in the picture, but his name was written or mentioned just below the photo with a tag “clicked by KUMAR.” Then, after he found his popularity on the rise, he realized he was now something of an expert. People now addressed him as if he were someone who knew well how to click pictures. Kumar became the go-to person for anyone who wanted to learn photography.

But yes, you may think, what about his group members? Did they still tease him? Yes, they did, but the intensity had decreased and the sting had gone out of it. And, if they needed any photographer for anything, the first person they called was none other than Kumar.

From this story we get a clear view of how to overcome ignorance and negligence by people. If you are ignored by others, nourish your skills, use your negativity to turn it into positivity. **Someone said, "If you die every day, try a day by living with a smile", then you will come to know, life is about living and dying but it doesn't mean it is always about living, or always about dying**.

See your environmental factors, what individuals need, how everything begins. Create, find and read the circumstances. Truly, on the off chance, you need to beat the dust, since somebody or a group consistently bothers you, or acts as a menace for you. They will be nothing, on the off chance that you have ability. Try to use your skills to fight them and win them over. Make your space between them just like Kumar did. If you really need respect, earn it by learning something or creating something. Otherwise, you may keep getting bullied, or teased. You have the time, see clearly.

THE DEATH

Two days ago, I was sitting on a broken bench by a river side. It was evening. I didn't have any fear of death. The peace and silence that come from death are so amazing that many can feel it. BUT, is it only from death? By the way, I don't even know how to swim. People always ask you this before and after your death, that WHO YOU ARE? A child? A teenager? An adult? Or a coward? People who surround you always ask mainly three questions from you. Parents ask you - Do you want to see us feeling proud of you? The whole family asks you - Do you want to see us walking with our heads down among the people of the society? And you would hear this from your teachers, family, friends - Are you wasting our effort and money? Do whatever we suggest. You don't have the brains to think. You will not be able to do what you think. You will do this, you will do that, you will drain our money, you will live and, well? What they don't say is, eventually, you will DIE. D-I-E, die.

I am 10 steps away. A voice interrupts, wait – what do you generally expect from yourself? If you are reading this then yes, I am not sharing news with you. A girl committed suicide just because she wasn't able to achieve her goal. A boy died after he jumped from the terrace. One hanged himself with a rope. There are many more. Do you want to be one of those headlines? Yes, for a few minutes you get a fearful imagination.

But truly said, it was an idiotic experience. Idiotic? Yes. Just because you are taking your situation very lightly, you are nothing. You don't have answers to those questions. Yes, you don't, until you know what you are escaping from, for years. Your likes, your passion, your dream, or you yourself?

So, I was sitting there and playing with my mind. Maybe it would have helped me understand something, but no, it didn't! People say, share your feelings, for when you share you feel relaxed. True, but not always. What if he or she uses it against you later? Yes, I know, he or she is my best friend, maybe one of the best friends. But still I want to keep it a secret from them. Should I write it out in my diary? But, what if someone reads it when I am not there? No, I am not negative, I just don't want to trouble anyone who thinks about my welfare. What if the reader, my well-wisher, gets impacted by all that negativity and then feel bad about me or worry for me or think that I am weak?

No, no, and no you are not thinking this, you are stuck to your old, conventional ideas that are stopping you from being brave and finding a good and helpful listener. You know you are weak and you don't want to show your real face. The truth is, you don't want to hurt yourself every day, you don't want to DIE. You want yourself to be respected and taken as normal when people get to know about you.

The river was looking at me, and seemed to be saying, "Come, I will take you with me, and then you will not get to hear anyone who can talk to you like that."

This is a story about me, if you are reading this then obviously you will get to know that I was weak one day. Yes, even today I am weak like you and many others. But what is the difference between you and me? Can you say it, that you are the one who can steal something from a store? Can you say it, you abuse your parents? Can you? Do you slap anyone? Do you hurt anyone? Do you think something mindlessly? Do you ever think about confessing your love? For some time, you hesitate to answer yourself just like me, because we really don't want to answer. This is not your fault, this is just what you were taught and you have seen in your surroundings. That is, if you do something wrong you will be punished. And, the bigger the mistake, the harder you will be punished. If you feel or even go beyond the rules that bind you within a boundary, it is obvious you will hide it or maybe it will become your deepest secret. No matter, it relates to love or your passion or your dream or your action. This is what I am trying to figure out, because it was going to be my second. Second what? If you are reading and listening to my words, then you know why I was there the second time.

Yes, the river side was quite mesmerizing and even the sunset was quite amazing. But as people said, try to share. Did anybody tell us how? I think no, and it is because those who experience this, those who have had a tough time, have faced intense situations, sometimes, it is hard for them to explain how it feels, and why we travel this way?

Our situation is like someone travelling in a boat - if you know how to swim, then you never sink until and unless someone grabs you from inside. Here, swimming denotes the safest way to go through the path you want to step onto. Let's take an example. If a girl's father has a good job and he gives his daughter a fixed weekly pocket money, then she can spend it on partying, or in her guitar classes. Maybe she wants to learn dancing or singing or something else. The pocket money is her swimming ability.

Let me help you with another example, a common one. If a boy has the ability to understand what's taught in class in one or two attempts then it can be safely concluded that he can do other things, too, at a higher speed compared to others who take more than two efforts to understand sometimes. This is what I called the **swimming ability**.

Now the second fact about travelling in that boat is the importance of maintaining balance. That is, travelling with an ideology that both sides should be given adequate attention. For this, you need to assume to yourself that you are the one who can do two things at a time. Take for a small example something that you usually do - while you are talking to an acquaintance on cellphone, the bell suddenly rings. It's someone on an errand, say the milkman. Well, you could continue the telephone conversation while still managing whatever odd job the milkman had come for. It means you have the balance. Just like that you need to maintain balance in your likes or passion with respect to your study or work. That is what I call **180-degree Balance**.

The third fact that was very important to learn was who you are? Where you are? And whether the step you are taking is correct or not? This fact can be defined by Navigation of the boat. Take an example of a person who never did anything in a proper manner. But one day, he learnt the trick of doing the same work better and faster. But then a day came when he realized he was merely working fast but skipping many things. Despite the faster work, he was not productive enough. And, there was another person who did a fixed work, but was never satisfied with his mechanical actions. He tried different ways to do it. One day, he took files on his head and entered the office. Everyone's eyes were attracted to him, a few said he was crazy, but some also appreciated him for his seeming craziness that had given him a fresh breath of fun. Another day, he clasped the files to his chest, in a bag, such that his hands were free and he could give someone tea first. Maybe that person was his boss. Even that day, someone appreciated while another called him crazy. On the third day, he was seen normally distributing the files. A few people asked him about his working style, but some still called him crazy. It is the navigation, that doesn't move with the speed of the flow of the water. You are on the boat so you have the right to choose directly. This navigation trick, I call it **the navigation-turn trick**.

Now to conclude this, the first and the last thing you have to know in this world is that no one ever cares about you really doing something in the right way or in the wrong way. No individual has the time to look after your every action till your death. If you die, they will cry for you, your closest ones, and if you live, they will talk to you maybe once a week, a month may be a year. After a few years, you shoulder the responsibilities of their lives and family. They can remember you but they don't give time into it. This is the harsh truth. Death is something beyond your imagination. Yes, you can decide to die, but you can also decide what to add in your life, and how to deal with the situation you are currently facing.

That river called me up and I sat down by its bank, put my legs inside the waters and sat for more than fifteen minutes. Then I realized, that's my start, even though I haven't experienced many things, I have many things to do. Then, the main thing I remembered was that I was out in the market, but got diverted to that river just because I did not even know who I am? Even my name was given by my parents. And, I will die after making my name worth a million.

...DON'T HAVE PATIENCE

We generally get tired of listening to this or that. Still, we have to keep patience. If you want something, have patience. If you are struggling with something, have patience. If you want to get rid of something, have patience, if you need true love, have patience. Did someone tell you, when the result came after you had your patience with you? Did someone help you in answering all your questions or did you, instead, hear many times, 'Wait for the right time, for time will answer your questions.'

Hey you there, yes, you who are reading this. My name is David. Yes, I know it is a simple middle class of the sons' names, which my father chose for me. I am one of the boys who were asked to have patience once, every day, for something or the other. I know what type of a guy I am, but what do I do? When I saw my friend's roller skates, I asked my father for a pair of them. He always said, have patience, he would buy them when he got his salary. It's two years now, my friend has a roller skate board, and I don't even have roller skates. Okay fine, it's so long now that, I've forgotten how much I'd have loved to have them, or imagined how it would look on my feet.

Then, another incident happened to me, in our programming class. We were working on something that I can't remember, because the day I started it, I left it the 4th day of it. Yes, it's not compulsory to do, so I left, why I should waste my time! People always say, save your time, so I am saving it, right? I am a nice player in 'Minecraft,' I own many things, after winning over so many new obstacles I made it. Now, I know what type of game it is, and I am enjoying it.

I think I was targeted by the time and fate, and I even shared it with my friends that time always tested me on having patience. But, why only me? So yes, let me share with you one more case - me and my girlfriend broke up. Reason? I didn't give time to the relationship. Maybe I was wrong in some places, and I think I was careless, or maybe I was rude. Or maybe she was wrong for me. Once, my best friend told me that being attracted to a girl is not love. Understanding her personally and then believing in each other leads to a perfect love story. And, even then, ups and downs are always a part of it. But, I didn't listen to him. Thankfully, he was still with me.

I know you sometimes think after reading my stories that aren't we the same? Or did you show less patience sometimes, but didn't want to share. If it happened to you, then, yes, we are the same.

But how to know you have less patience. Well, you can find that out, too. Wait, let me help you. I am going to ask a few questions. Just write the answers on paper, or remember your answer. The easy one, ha-ha.

Here go the questions - Have you ever tried to discover something but left it in the middle just because you don't know how to do it? The next question, have you ever tried social media to meet new people just to talk to them. What if the person you want to talk to doesn't reply to you? Do you see yourself at the very bottom when being compared to others in any work, project, or anything? Have you ever made mistakes after mistakes? And, have you ever felt that you would never be able to clear them all or correct them? Do you feel that having loved someone but felt them to be out of your reach? There are many more, but I will not bore you. So, the fact I was talking about, is if you answered, YES, once or more, then, yes, you have less patience. Harsh truth but yes, it is. Don't skip reading, complete it first. Even this will be another mistake of not completing a small story at a time. I know you don't want to do it.

So, why did I ask you this question? While answering this question, have you heard any voices inside your head? Have you just felt something? I know you have, but if you have not, then go back to that paragraph and read again, trying to answer those questions truly. So, if you are with me, then I am going to answer a few of your questions, like how to deal with patience, how to understand it? Wait, this is the second part, that is just a basic, and the question will be why you have less patience? Yes, it's not easy to listen to you, as you know I don't have any power to listen from pages, ha-ha. But yes, if I am not wrong, then, you are with my assumption, and I can help you with it.

THE ANSWERS

According to my browser, I mean Google, **patience means the quality of being able to stay calm and not get angry, especially when there is a difficulty or you have to wait a long time**. But I think the meaning of this word must be **the way you are tested by your own decisions**. This means that most of the decisions, are always taken by you, no matter i small or big, but you do. So, it is the time which passes after your decision that tests your decision. If you are keen about it, or you have just taken a decision after being motivated, or just after having seen someone working on it, so you also need to know how to work on it. And, seeing someone doing and being motivated to work on something is not a bad thing. Even working on something differently, after seeing someone else doing it, is also a good thing. But the hard truth is, did you take a proper measure, or, in what condition you had to do it? How are you going to make it? Or, say, where are you going to use it?

If I think, that you have taken all these measures, but, still there is a mistake always made by everyone, even I do, your friends do, your parents do, how much effort does it cost? How much time does it take? One might have been working on it, because one needed it, one might have some issues, or one might wish to change something by which one will invent something, anything. But you? You were just motivated by him; you just saw him working on it, so you wanted to do it too. There is a big myth, save your time, it's useful, but no one says from where? The answer is here. Do you think why people say you need to work on your passion or you need to work on something you like the most? They directly or indirectly say that you will connect yourself with time and that will help you increase your PATIENCE. Let's take your example. You are a content creator, then you know you get tired of many things, mostly editing, because if you are 40% done and the system crashes or your editing software shuts down, you just lose your mind, but you know you need to do it, and you do. And if you are a writer, then it's obvious you will make mistakes while writing or even delivering your views, but after hours of hard work, days, nights, you do manage. Just like these two, I have many more examples, but I know you are intelligent. So, **if you need to be confident in Patience, don't take time, you need to buy time. Make your decision clean and clear after thinking over the questions I discussed above. You will enrich your patience levels after this**.

By the way, sorry for the lie, **I was quite impatient.** I am fine now, because I know the answers. Still I make mistakes related to my decision. Just like I do , you will also make mistakes, decision making has its own chapter, many writers have already worked on it, but what I am saying, take a decision, but don't be a fool. And yes, I am in a relationship with my second girlfriend, we understand each other, although I was working on a programme, I was doing great, I tried to make a game and I knew I would do it. Because I Have Patience.

CLOTHES AND YOUR SKIN (RACISM)

There was a girl who generally wore a crop top and jeans, from which we could guess that she was from a big city. Shall we consider from where she was? Or do we just need to go ahead with this story? I think I need to share everything about her. Maybe it would garner some sympathy from you. She was a resident of Delhi, India. After the serious lines above, I think you would get the impression that she was a modern type of girl? Oh no, nowadays every girl loves to wear crop top and jeans. Yes, it's the western culture, and moreover it holds you up when you are living in a city and where you are dealing with the crowd who look up to modernization and transformation as a change.

So, hi! This is your writer here, you can think of me as an anonymous blog writer who generally worked sporadically, brilliantly and often controversially for a few sites. While working in the current modernization scenario, I was attracted to a girl. She was well-dressed, considering the western culture. Because as you look into the Indian culture, you get to know more often about the trends and the dressing - it directly said that females should cover three-fourth of their bodies. But like always, many people have pointed out that uncountable movements have taken place over time, and while girls need to be protected, we also need to give them space to open up. We need to give them space where they could feel their own freedom like their male counterparts.

So, time and trends have shifted to the phase of acceptance of the traditions of western countries. How could accepting any trend and tradition be wrong for anyone? Would this answer be so tough to rely on? Not everyone, but many of us still don't want to see any change, or would never like, especially girls, to stand next to us like just another usual human being. Now, the question was how clothes could be related to gender equality. The answer was very simple. Did you see a girl who was in a sari and said that she didn't know about cooking? They know it, right? Because they are educated, or even if they aren't, still they know, but the fact is: what thought revolved around in your heads? It's all about conventional thinking. The general society talks thus, "Who's that girl and why she's wearing that t-shirt, a crop top, jeans, or shorts?" Maybe someone doesn't agree with me. But the fact I want to point out is, a girl is not a product. I am not raising my voice on behalf of the girls, but I just saw a girl getting differentiated on the basis of her clothes. How? Let's see inside this story.

This was the same girl I was attracted to, as I mentioned above. Yes, because of her beauty. Oh no, no, you get the answer, I was attracted to her figure. She was 5'5 tall, fair skin, and she wore a red crop-top and blue jeans, which is such a nice colour combination. I was sitting in a street-side corner of McDonald's and watched her across the glass wall. Her moves were simply the killer ones. But as she entered, I consciously heard a guy talking to his friends that she was so hot and they were saying what other guys would do if she would be their girlfriend and other such ridiculous talks. Listening to them, my brain burst out at the degradation of humanity! What they were thinking about her was so wrong. They were not good for our country and they could even become rapists down the line! Yes, I know, I was exaggerating! True? But the next moment, my mind came across a few questions. A few minutes before what was *I* thinking about her? What was *I* just imagining? What sort of words had *I* used for her? If we look at it from a different viewpoint, these words were not even bad. If her friends told her that she was looking hot or sexy, or given hundreds of other compliments that would easily be accepted by her. But the problem is that if you are a stranger, first you need to respect her, then, come closer to her, like a friend, best friend or may be boyfriend, and then shower her with those compliments freely.

While these thoughts were running through my head, she entered the restaurant, and surprisingly, took a seat next to me. So, openly I told her with politeness, "Sorry miss, but as you entered inside, I couldn't help but notice you. You are looking beautiful, in fact hot in this dress. This may sound odd to you coming from a stranger, but I am openly expressing what I felt." To this, she replied, "Thank you, Mister but may I know why are you trying to impress me?" Then, we started talking together and eventually sat at the same table. Then one of her friends joined us, the one for whom she had come to McDonald's in the first place.

There it was, what we saw, the way of talking, the way of expressing feelings could change someone's thinking about you. In fact, conversational education must be taught from the age of 7 and 8 onwards. But most people forget these basic soft skills and

do not pass it on to their children. In this story, we could see the girl was already educated, she knew how to talk to people, how to reply and how to handle themselves. Mostly, that's not seen. But we need that world where people have the good sense of knowing what they are doing.
So, yes, she accepted my compliment. That particular time, I was the nicest guy. No, I was one of the nicest guys, who talked openly and he knew how to respond even through his body language, his tone, his way of talking. All these attract people. Yes, these are called soft skills. If you are faking then definitely you will be caught some time, you will lose trust, and you will lose your image. And, even if you are physically unattractive to someone, if you have that amazing skill, people will reach out to you. I can sense that you felt uneasy with this statement, so let's go back to the story and see what this story is teaching us.
I said hi to her friend, and then I went to the counter for our order. You know how McD's is - the tables are not that far apart and even from the counter I could overhear their conversation. I heard the new girl ask her friend, "Hey, you didn't tell me about this male friend of yours?"
"He isn't a friend. I just met him 15-20 minutes ago."
"What? What's wrong with you? How could you share a table with a dark, strange guy? I am not comfortable sitting here. What's wrong with your taste in boys?"

The girl I had befriended said that I had given honest compliments about her dressing and she was impressed; in addition, I had talked to her openly.

Then, in between, her friend said with surprised eyes, "What will your other friends say? That you reject people on social media, and talk to strangers who are dark, who look strange, who don't..."

She had to cut herself off as I reached back to the table just then and said, "You can take something."
I didn't blame the girl, for she was not wrong. Many people treat others on the basis of their looks and skin colour, as we do.

At that moment, somebody called her friend and she whispered in her ears and said bye to her. And she left us alone together. Then she decided...... ok, wait, why do I keep referring to her as she? Her name was Shayna. Shayna told me that her friend had left her, and she couldn't go back home right now. So, she asked me if I was free for an hour. Well, I replied to her that I was free for 2 hours, after which I had to attend my class. Thus, it happened that Shayna and I were together in a park, walking and talking.
Before saying bye to each other, she asked me suddenly, "I know that many girls wore western dresses just because they needed attention, and liked to get compliments. Why did you compliment only me? For there were other girls inside."

I replied, "I know there were many modern girls inside, but if you hadn't sat next to me, or if you happened to be with someone, then maybe there were least chances of my saying even a word to you."

She laughed, then I said, "I don't like girls in sari." Wearing a sari doesn't show the openness and freedom of a girl. To which she replied, "I wear mostly Indian dresses. Even then, I feel I have all the freedom. You'd better stop judging females on the basis of their looks and clothing. They need freedom, and the society can't bind them with tradition." She was happy that I gave a compliment to her, but what if she wore sari and would I again compliment her? Maybe not. Females are okay when they are called with their names, not colour, they feel protected when they are introduced with their skills not dressing. Stop the racism of clothes relating to a girl. Clothes were designed for everyone. If you are going among people wearing a jersey then girls also should have that basic freedom.

She added that racism is not only about skin colour. She said she wanted me to talk, because my skills had introduced me already, not my skin colour. Just like that, she and other females needed respect for their skills, abilities, not only their looks and their dresses. If they think they look beautiful in western dresses then they should have that freedom, and even if they are wearing a sari, they should have a feeling of freedom and a space for themselves. Then we said bye to each other, and yes, we shared our social media links.

That girl, I was really inspired by her. I thought only skin colour created racism issue but no, the situation was tougher for females because of this issue called the **racism of clothes**. So, now I like girls irrespective of their choice of dress be it Indian or western. The only point I consider is whether they are having their space, and are accepted for their individual attributes and abilities. After all, as far as external appearances go, I am one of the dark-skinned people, too.

ON THE ROADS – MEMOIRS

A Few real incidents happened to or were experienced by the writer on the roads, and have been described in a story form here.

If you know me, then it is okay, if you do not, then let me tell you I don't want anyone to take me out for a walk. I am one of the useless people who are generally found in the streets anyway, and I hope you are not going to ask when. It's all the god-forbidden hours! If you want to meet me, just fix it and I will join you. So, my dear readers, if you have already gone through the first two sections, I hope this section will tell you about me. No not really, for you need to extract it out - the info about me and what type of person I am. This section was written on the basis of my general travel in cities, on roads, or anywhere else, where I found something to learn. Is it amazing? Somehow it is, and if you want to see the little things, which I never skip, then start reading this section.

“DONT KILL ME, YOU ARE EDUCATED”

In the morning I woke up late, I think around 7:30am. My room was messed up as I had worked late in the night and went off to sleep at 3 am. Due to the panic of waking up late, I left my breakfast unfinished. I took it in a lunch box and ran for a shared taxi. In Mumbai, I had found several public transport options to travel from one place to another. The city was very crowded and busy as always. Mumbai is really very challenging, and is also termed as the City of Startups. I got out of the taxi, and paid the driver 100 bucks. While in the process of economic exchange, he saw panic on my face. My eyes were demanding complete rest but it was too late for me to take a nap. The morning sun stared at me with its diagonal eyes, showering unbearable heat. This is every working person's and student's reality. The tags given to this Mumbai city- 'Financial Capital of India', 'City of Dreams', 'City of Lights', and the list goes on, were just the ironies of life because of its people living there. You would rarely see people stopping for any incident or situation. No sooner did I reach my destination than I jumped out of the seat and started walking hastily, not running. I decided not to cross that BLACK AND WHITE ILLUSION on the road to reach the other side. Instead, I used the underground subway. While I was counting the number of stairs and was about to descend the last of the staircases, the cracked enamel of the stairs dismantled from its mass into small pebbles and came up off its tread (upper part of the steps of stairs). I pushed inside and in a microsecond I was thinking whether I could fix it. What if anyone doesn't notice it? They say to err is human, I and justified this saying by making a wrong statement, "Who cares?" Maybe I was too rude? Maybe it was the thought of many of us? Maybe we could get used to these problems? But to counter it, I have a question: do we really have no time to fix our general problems? I don't know what your answer will be but I think we need to halt for a while for lifestyle quality to get better.

So, I was heading towards the bus stand, but what happened to me there changed my thoughts, way of thinking, and even my belief in humanity.

I met a beggar, his name was Chand. He was a rag picker but a few months ago he had been expelled from the company where he worked as a low-wage worker. My conversation with him changed me.

"Hello!" said the beggar, "For the sake of God give me something to eat."
I ignored him.
He repeated again, adding, "Please, I want something to eat."
I went back to his statement - there was no scope of confusion, he was not asking for any money, he just wanted some food.
I replied, "I have bread-jam, do you want to eat?"
He nodded his head with gleeful approval.
I gave him a smile and saw him eating. Clearly, I thought, he was hungry for maybe more than 24 hours. But at that moment, I asked him out of curiosity, "Why didn't you ask for the money instead of edible things?"
He replied, and his answer blew my mind. He said, "I am hungry and I am experiencing weakness, I need to deal with it first. And if you want to know why, then my answer is, asking for money will not give me something to end my hunger instantly. I am not like other beggars. One day I was a worker, too. Even these days I earn from my bit jobs, but can't fill my stomach. So, getting ignored by people hurts me a lot. When I go to the shops they beat me or push me out. Once, they didn't even accept my money (he cried as he said this, but continued) as their mindset says that I am dirty or I belong to a class of untouchables."
"This is the truth of every nook of our world. The way people treat each other is indeed a matter of agony and despondency. Few beggars make it a habit to even teach their own children to beg

on streets. Few get beaten up, etc. Yes, I am not saying that we were correct, no we were not. I would better say **TRUST** died long ago. So going through this long way, I simply thought to ask you for food just to end my hunger. THANK YOU."

So that moment I was totally lost in his words, the way he answered my question. I remember his last line. He said, "You are going to someone who will be a helper, even if you are going to be educated, therefore, in future, don't forget we need help, for everyone is not the same."

SLEEP, PUNCTURE and HUNGRY

During the day time, I generally decide to roam or move about somewhere. Not that I do not have a packed schedule. I do, but I know how to manage my time and satisfy my craving to travel. So on a busy day, Monday, in the morning, I was planning to go somewhere to meet someone for a work-related discussion, or a meeting, as we call it. I got ready, had breakfast and went out on the roads walking. I took out my mobile to look for the shortest and the easiest path to reach my destination. Everyone knows that Google Maps is getting more advanced by the day, and so I followed all its instructions. It mentioned the direction and also what vehicle/ transport I should take. I found I had to go for the best choice, that is, an auto-rickshaw (3-tire vehicles used as a public transport in India), called 'auto' commonly.

So, I started looking for a vacant auto-rickshaw. Yes, it's obvious you will get a vacant auto in the morning very easily, but if you are in the city of Mumbai, which is an overcrowded place, every auto is occupied. Finally, I found one where the driver was cleaning its seat. I asked him, and luckily he agreed to take me to my destination. Well, I was so used to hearing a no from them that it was really a shocking reply. Then I saw him check both his rear tires. Then he started his auto, prayed to god and started the ride. In the middle of the journey, I asked him why he was checking out the tires as they had looked perfectly fine to me. He said, and I quote, "Sir, we are drivers, our homes run on the money earned by this transport, and many nights I spend sleeping inside it. So I check it thoroughly every morning, to confirm that everything is working. And I especially check the rear tires because they hold my weight. This auto is my partner, and it gives me a place to sleep. In return, if I take care of it then my hunger and all other needs will get fulfilled."

What a beautiful thought! I so appreciated his deep emotions. It’s very nice to know about human beings, what they care for, with whom they are attached, and what it means to their lives.

"…. THE BEST I SERVE THE BEST WISHES I WILL GET"

I had an experience when I was on the streets of HINJEWADI, PUNE. There was a street hawker whose stall was known for his delicious Dhabeli. It was at trend so it will be better to mention it with respect, (hashtag) Dhabeli. As usual, I was in Pune to attend a few meetings and also for my college work.

I have made many friends, mostly those who are older than me, and I like their support, kindness and care. As I was staying in Hinjewadi, a locality known as IT Hub/IT Street because many well-known IT companies have been set up there. More than 400+ big and small companies can be found in Hinjewadi. The people I met were generally of the working age or businessmen, no matter big or small, and for whatever they do.

So ahead to the topic I was focusing about that Dhabeliwala. So, one day I was extremely hungry. I got up from my bed, checked my wallet and found it had a mere 100 bucks. And that was enough for me to eat any street food. First of all, I would say that it was a great experience at that place, at 7 in the evening. I looked his working speed and yes, the crowd surrounding his stall. By the time my chance came, the crowd had thinned a bit. Concerned for him, I asked him to take a few minutes' rest and drink some water. He said, "Thank you sir, but the better I serve you the better wishes you will give." His words just grabbed my heart and held it for a few seconds without pumping. All I could say was, *"To tyachya kamat changla aahe aani to khup dayalu aahe."*

I know you didn't understand the above words. They were spoken in Marathi, the regional language of Maharashtra, a western Indian state. It means, "He is good at his work and he is a kind person."

We generally blame our situation, we often say had this been such and such I'd have fared better in life, and so on. If we scrutinize this Dhabeli seller's work, we will wonder what he may be thinking of, about growing his business or buying a shop or may be having a restaurant. Yes? Okay so, whenever I looked at his face I saw fatigue but with a smile glazing through it. Maybe it will be better, maybe it will be good for him when his situation improves. What I think is that someone starting from zero to hundred can feel greater satisfaction than the one who got directly to a hundred. Because he will never know the journey to hundred, he can't even experience that fun of struggle! Through his words, the Dhabeliwala easily conveyed to me that he accepted his situation and that he was working for a better life. The experience of making tasty food, even holding the crowd with his speed could help him to grow. And he knew very well he was the one who was very happy.

THE FEAR OF GETTING LOST

I never know why I love to travel, but this time the experience was different. I visited Delhi in 2011, but still, even after 7 years, I could remember the lanes, the roads, and few buildings. I am quite old enough really. I have the freedom to go out of the house. The years 2018 and 2019 were spent in doing experiments and taking risks. My very first risk was taken by me when I learnt to talk to strange girls. Yes, it's hard to ask something, but if you want something, a favour or help, you need to take that risk. And that experiment really increased my confidence level and helped me a lot in Delhi. That day I was out with my bag, and I planned to cover the 'Rajiv Chowk' area and the places around the Hauz Khas Metro station. Generally, I depend on the Google map, and I love to explore places on my own. Mainly, I look for landmarks and roam about like a *banjara*. It is funny but it is a really amazing experience at the same time. Yes, if I get company, I feel very grateful, but most people cannot bear me. Umm, yes, according to what I heard from a few people, there are some who don't like my company for they like to go to glitzy places and hangouts. It hurt me a lot in the past, and so I came to love my own company. Now, I walk long distances, I explore things, I meet new people, and animals, too. And I am really grateful to those people who enjoy my company.

While walking on the streets, I felt many times that I was getting lost in the city. However, one line always helps me to stay motivated in those confusing times - if you get lost in the lanes or roads you are still going to remain in Delhi. So there I was!

That day I found many people who helped me, even those who passed comments because of my simple clothes and loneliness. But as I was out for exploring things and making my own map, so I simply ignored them with a pleasant smile. Really, I don't understand why people tease those who have anything lacking at that present moment.

So, as I was out, I re-filled my metro card at the Nirman Vihar Metro station. Then I proceeded with my wanderings. I checked the route, but I was not quite familiar with the various networks of the Delhi Metro, what with their violet line, or the yellow line. I was new there but still I knew people were surely going to help me. I just had to ask. And I found a man who helped me by explaining the route. Then I met a regular traveller of that route, who helped. By then I was on my own. I was now on the road, and I was looking for the road to the Lodhi Garden, which is a famous garden in Delhi known for its beauty and history of Mohammad Shah's Tomb. Including that, there are many things to see, and it is one of the popular tourism spots, too. So, I thought I will go there and explore everything. Now I was 3 km away from that place, and lo! My internet got stuck and I got lost in a housing society.

I was inside there, and it was really quite hilarious, for I was going round and round the 5 buildings that looked just the same. Even all the paths were looking the same, too. In frustration, I sat on a see-saw. Thankfully, the children playing there helped me in getting out of the society. They asked about me, for they had never seen me before. Few of the parents got alert considering I was a stranger, but when I described my situation, each and every individual, child or adult, laughed out loud. Then 2 little girls and 1 boy helped me to reach the exit gate, and I thanked them profusely. Even for those 15 to 20 minutes I enjoyed the social interactions. Then as I was figuring out a few buildings shown in the maps, I found three girls walking ahead of me. So, I ran for like 100 meters behind them and then requested them for directions to reach the place. They showed me the route with all the turns. And lo and behold the coincidence! I saw them again near the gate of Lodhi Garden! It seemed as if they had also been planning to go there. But you see, I was on my own, exploring, reading building names, clicking pictures.

And after roaming here and there and enjoying every new moment, I came back home. That day I got lost three times, I got tired, I felt frustrated sometimes, but from all that, I learnt something. The path never decides where you have to go. You decide where you really want to go. If you found yourself, then sit down, or take a pause, and see around, try to understand the way you got stuck inside, for that is probably the only way you will come out. The fear of getting lost is obvious for you, but if you are out for exploring things, take it also as an exploration. Because then you will not really get lost. Besides, as J. R. R. Tolkien says, 'Not all who wander are lost.'

WHAT DO YOU LIKE TO SEE IN A GIRL?

What do you like in a girl? When you learn from your experiences, you realize you have learnt much more than the words. And sometimes, we learn from other's experiences, too, and that changes our lives in some aspects. Like you learn from others' mistakes, and do not repeat them after seeing how it impacted them. Now it reminds me of the time I was sitting next to a man when travelling to Kerala with my friends. Due to some reason, I was sitting two compartments away from them, and there were several other passengers sitting on their respective seats or berths of the train. They were talking and discussing on many topics, and one of them was raised by the guy sitting right next to me. While continuously listening to them, another chap asked me to join them, and I thought, well, why not! So, I became a part of their discussion on few topics like business models and work fields. We even had question-answer rounds. Few fell in the mid-twenties to mid-thirties, and they were not from the same field. So, even the task of introducing each other had become an intriguing task.

Then they raised an interesting topic among them, after having disposed of strong topics related to experiences. That topic was related to the feelings and the connections between people, and how time plays an important role in making connections. And how why relations were destroyed and yet we clung to them. Then a sub-topic was raised, related to why opposite genders were attracted to each other? This time I got a chance to speak, too. Before I shared my experiences and opinion, I asked a basic question -

How many of them had first felt the attraction for someone before becoming a part of their life?

? Like we can say we become friends, then we get deeply involved and enter into a relationship. This develops into a strong relationship to which we give a name or rather we announce, "We are in love with each other." Everyone agreed with me, and even you readers are also going to agree with me.

Then I continued that this happened because many of us really needed someone with whom we could share, to whom we could say I am not alone. It's a fact that sometimes we never want a relationship because we know we will spoil it, that we can't handle it. Still, I know you have heard a basic statement from someone or the other, "Pyaar to bas ho jata hai." This line was in the Hindi language, and it means, "Love just happens unconditionally."

This is true because it has never been conclusively proved that there is a chemical reaction after seeing someone, and we decide that person is going to be my life partner after that. Yes, we say few things like, he or she is not my type, or I don't make up things with him or her or he or she can't understand me. This is because as we are born alone, as individuals, we are raised as individuals, and then maintaining 'I' plus one life is not easy for everyone.

And exactly for this reason, time remains our teacher. Break-ups are not meant for spoiling other's life, or saying he or she was wrong. It's about yes, you learn many things from that, you know what and how to say things to the next person, how to prepare yourself so that you can match better with that person, and many more things. Don't abuse someone, don't say bad words or do bad. Everything has its own ups and downs. Yes, if someone has planned to spoil someone's life, better get rid of that person by taking a few measures.....

I have the quality of talking well, and all of them were quite impressed. They wondered how I had acquired all this knowledge and I replied that I read people, and I wrote things about these topics. But we somehow got diverted from the topic. Then I asked a man sitting next to me what he saw in a girl or rather what he liked to see in a girl?

That man worked in a company and he was with his girlfriend, and they both were batch-mates first. So, I think that man was not quite free to talk that day. It was a hilarious situation but, yes many of us controlled ourselves and then listened to him. We questioned everyone else. When I replied, listening to my words, they said, "You will surely get a girl." Then everyone raised another topic, that what type of girl, I will get, which was really uncomfortable for me, because I was not prepared for that. But something that one of my co-passengers said was so profound that each one of us got pulled deep inside his lines and thoughts. He said that first of all, even today, being a girl is a tough job, if we look at the general way of living in India. He continued that he had seen his sister learning so many things in addition to the other basics as compared to him and had to do much more than what he was supposed to do.

Times are changing, everyone has talked about equal rights, but generally, his sister was confident that she did not need any aid or special assistance or reservations, for she could achieve what she wanted based on her abilities. She felt that by offering these said benefits, the government was showing women as weak and dependent. .

Many families who were civilized and well-educated understood these things irrespective of where they were living or what they were working at. That training means that many of us from either gender have been taught right from schools that we have to maintain a boundary. But no one has the rights to ask questions regarding those boundaries, because our past, that is, our elders, don't want to answer. And those who do, when there is openness inside a family, there is openness in the society, that society grows faster, because when there are clean and clear questions and answers then there will be growth. According to him, what he liked to see in a girl were only three things: that she should be open and knows her right to question that will increase her confidence too, that is not confined to skin and colour. . Like many girls get enraged as any topic is raised against girls, without checking what the issue is going on. This creates divisions, and researching and learning always make both the genders polite. Such people never react in the first place. And the last point he put across was that he needed a girl who should respect him and give him a chance to speak. That last point again raised a round of laughter among us, for after saying that he looked at his girl-friend. And then she was like, “Didn’t I give you the space to talk? Look how mean he is to me?” This could be an end in any discussion, but one point we always have to consider -is a girl’s beauty more important than the way she cares for you? Society has done this discussion so many times, it teaches us, but what? That is a big topic, and I don’t want to deliver a speech like those we had to prepare for our assembly during the school days.

GENERAL STORIES

This section has stories related to the society. The style of writing is quite natural and reflects the general lifestyle of people around us.

For this section I will thank the people and the society, among whom I grew up. Er, I mean I am still growing up. I am grateful that I have learnt many things ever since I was a 6 years old child. With a crazy and creative mind, I have been an observer, and, though it was not that good, now I am constantly working on my writing, sketching and observational skills. This section of stories doesn't have many stories compared to the other sections of this book, but this section tells you, directly how I have seen people? How human beings respond to each and every action, doesn't matter either mentally or physically. The craziest part of this section is THE EXPERIENCE.

The stories are quite long in this section, but they have parts, so make sure you are giving sufficient time to this. The best part of these stories is the plot and the characters. They are going to show you or deliver to you the meaning of the story and keep up the interest inside. Take a bottle of water and understand your society.

PHOTGRAPHS, STORIES AND IF HE ASKS FOR...

It was night like always, but that day Anand was not prepared for sleep. He was just imagining the girl who would be his girlfriend. Anand loved to travel, and for three days, he had been dreaming about something beautiful. Three days ago, he and his friend were discussing about how they wanted a friend with whom they would want to be very close, and with whom they wanted to meet as soon as possible. Anand was habitually shy, and he only wanted a friend to share his thoughts with, no matter how crazy. He wanted to sit on a rock and count stars with her. Yes, he needed a female friend.

That day, he had his dinner and went back to his room. Let's see how his room looks: all the four walls were filled with photographs of roads, night-time sky, moon, daylight, fields, and mountains. He also had his own photos that he had clicked. In fact, when he went for school trips, he made sure to capture moments. All his photos were well-organized in their places and all the photos were interlinked with each other. Yes, each photo had its own story. Whenever Anand went to sleep he always checked Google to enlist places he wanted to see.

That day, he lay down and started thinking about a girl, about how he'd first meet her, what his first lines would be to her? What he would do as a favor for her? With such thoughts and imaginations, he drifted asleep.

Every time he wanted to imagine something nice, he failed. Now, his nights were spoiled because of his sleep. Then a day came when his family decided to enjoy the winter vacations in the famous hill station of Sikkim in Northeast India.

He was too excited about that. He planned everything for his travelling, the camera, the batteries, and the bag in which he kept his diary, a teddy, few pencils, and his pocket money. He took clothes that he wanted to wear while travelling. They were planning to go to Gangtok, Sikkim's capital city. They had to travel from Meghalaya to Gangtok. During this exciting journey, he forgot his dreams and imaginations because he loved to travel and there was nothing more important than that.

They were going to travel by bus, and it was going to be a road journey because of Anand's love for photography. Besides, they were a middle-class family, and booked the simple bus tickets for their trip. In his family, there were just three people - his parents and Anand. Anand and his family were not from the Northeastern states, they were from Delhi. It was because his father worked here that his full family had settled here.

“Did you take your slippers?” That was his mother.

“I hope so because my bag was already overfull,” Anand replied.

“I know exactly what is filling up your bag! Okay fine, I will cross-check your bag. Go and eat your meal, we have to leave in one hour,” said his mother.

Anand had his meal, and everyone was ready for their trip. Soon they were out and waiting at the bus stand for the bus to come. After 15 to 20 minutes, their bus came. Anand ran for the window seat while his parents sat one row behind. His father asked him for his bag, to keep on the top shelf, where bags of other passengers were kept, but he refused. He had some precious stuff with him that he needed while traveling. The seat next to him was empty for a few passengers were to be let in only after 200 kms.

The hills along the road were too beautiful, and soon he had started with his camera, capturing few images like a tall tree bowing to a smaller and one with the sun just in the middle. Then he clicked a picture of the height his bus was at. He took photos of turnings, and of fruit sellers and stunning vistas. Then when he reached the place where they were to have lunch, he took an extra battery with him. As per the rule, the bus had to stop here for about half an hour. However, with stones on the road having damaged two of the bus tires, the driver and conductor were hoping to repair the same during this period. The passengers left their respective seats, with few people talking to each other, strangers trying to make friends. Anand was quite excited because he got many stories to capture, like an old woman selling fruits, the driver changing the large bus tires, his father kissing his mother’s forehead, monkeys snatching food from people or playing with some boys, beautiful hills, a waterfall, and then a beautiful girl. A smiling girl wearing a flower in her hair. Almost unconsciously, he clicked 10 to 15 pictures of that girl, and then

he stopped. He took another angle then clicked two more pictures hiding from her, while she was setting her hair.
Then all of a sudden someone tapped on his back. He turned around and saw there was a beautiful lady, about his mother's age.
"Yes ma'am, how can I help you?" Anand said.
The lady said, "I am the mother of the girl whose pictures you are clicking."
Nervous, Anand started stuttering that he was just clicking pictures innocently, that he loved to click pictures, that he clicked pictures just for the sake of the stories behind them, and he would have gone on and on when the lady just smiled and stopped him.
"Hey, hey, hey, child, don't worry. I am not mad at you. All I say is, if you really want to click her pictures go and ask her," she said.
Surprised, Anand asked, "You will not mind? I mean if I will click her pictures?"
"Her name is Ruhani. And I know your father because he is a friend of my husband's. When I saw him, I remembered. I talked to him and he told me about you, that I will see you here clicking pictures. So don't worry, kid," she said.
Now Anand was relieved, and walked over to Ruhani. She was roaming about, looking for flowers in a flower shop.
"This yellow flower will best suit your dress and beauty," Anand said, putting his camera down.
'Who are you? Have we met before?" Ruhani asked.
"I hope so, that's why I know you, Ruhani," he said.
"HEY! Wait, how do you know my name?" she asked.
"Hey, you were the one who asked if we'd met before. So I replied to you," he said with a smile.
"I'm really very curious how you know my name?" she said in confusion.
Anand laughed, and said, "Wait! Wait, don't get so mystified, you don't know me, I know that. Just a few minutes ago your mother

met me and she told me your name when I was clicking your pictures."

"What? Why were you clicking my pictures, and why would my mother tell you my name? She's strict with strangers," she said.

In politeness Anand replied, "You are beautiful, that's why I clicked your pictures. Don't worry, maybe your mother is strict with strangers, but I am not one. She knows my father through your father, that's why she came to me."

After listening to Anand, Ruhani relaxed.

"By the way, my name is Anand", he continued.

"Since you already know my name, so, hello Anand," she said.

Then she asked him about his camera and his love of clicking pictures, wondered whether he clicked only beautiful girls or other stuff as well. To this he replied with confidence, though with an endearing little stutter, that he was not restricted to pretty faces, that he clicked anything with stories, anything with feelings, and anything that attracted him, no matter how bad it was.

Hearing his reply she smiled, and said that she thought he was new to that mountains. He revealed that he was from Shillong (capital of Meghalaya), from a busy town. But being a towner, he wanted to see a place from where he could make a short story with big pictures. Yes, the mountains, winds, roads, rivers, waterfalls, everyone speaks. We just have to listen to them, for sometimes they sound as deep as our heart beats. From his words, she found that Anand was an explorer at heart, and she liked this character of him. Curious, he asked Ruhani about her likes and dislikes and where she was going? She shared that she was living in a small town, where she studied in a Christian school and there her mother was the English teacher. She and her mother were planning a visit to their native place in New Jalpaiguri in West Bengal.

They had a long conversation, though even in between those moments, Anand clicked many pictures of the mountains, nature, people around him and even a few clicks of Ruhani.

Just then the bus horn rang out, and he said reluctantly that he had to leave now, with his parents. Waving goodbye to Ruhani he disappeared in a rush in the crowd of passengers. Ruhani smiled and started searching for her mother whom she saw buying snacks from a stall. In a few minutes from then, they, too, stepped into their bus.

"You? Again?" Ruhani asked in wonder.
Anand turned back and he said, "Yes I am, but you?"
They were both confused but after a few seconds, they laughed out. So, her mother was sitting across the aisle, and Ruhani exchanged her seat with the man who was sitting next to Anand. Ruhani found that Anand was replacing the battery of his camera. She got interested and asked him to show her pictures that he had clicked.
Anand replied, "This is my gallery and only I have the right to see the pics. But if you want to see, you'll have to do something that I want you to do."

Ruhani looked confused but a smile glowed on her face.

She said, "What do I have to do for seeing my own pictures, Mr. photographer!"

Anand took a small sheet of, paper, made horns of it and asked her to wear them over her hairs so he could click 1-2 pictures. She laughed, and flatly refused to do so.
Then with a big smile, he said, "Think once before taking a decision."
She accepted that, and taking the paper horns from him, she wore them and got several pictures clicked. And while she called him a cheater, she accepted he was a clever one too, at the same time. But then he kept up his side of the bargain and showed her all his photos. She liked every picture he had clicked, few of them with amazing stories behind them - a man holding is son on his back, for he didn't have hands, so his son was plucking out fruits from a

tree. Then there was a pic in which an old woman was walking with 3 heavy containers of water. There was a picture in which a cute child was keenly observing a lollipop's attractive color. And there were many others. But the pictures she was most attracted to were hers. More than 50 of her photos were there in his gallery. In one pic, she found herself smiling, then in another she was kind of setting or playing with her hair. In another pic, she was just turning around, and the moment that he had captured that pic was so beautiful it looked as if the sunlight was kissing her body. Once she saw all the pictures, she looked up to him, then smiled and took a deep breath. Anand was excited. Why did she look at him and smile like that? Did she like him? Then suddenly, he said to himself, 'You are an idiot, why would she like you?'

While he was talking to himself, she offered him chips from her packet. But he hesitated before taking it. Unexpectedly, she grabbed his hand, put it inside the packet and said, "If you feel like eating, just pick it up and eat, you idiot!" He laughed and nodded his head in agreement. He felt her hand to be very soft, and much more interesting than the chips. He thought he was just going crazy about her, but felt the need to hide his feelings from her. They had a very amazing conversation while travelling, during which he introduced her to his family. Then they talked about various topics like studies, teachers, school life, hobbies, likes, dislikes, people, etc. While they were going through those topics, Ruhani stopped him and asked what type of people he wanted around himself. That is, what type of people he liked? After thinking much about this question, he said that he generally didn't know what type of people he found around him, because whenever he clicked pictures, he had seen different faces, different personalities, and different mindsets. But what he liked about a person was their clear aim to do something in life or their vision of life related to their hobbies. He or she must understand that real life is different from a virtual one lived inside a device, that virtual life inside devices was manmade, to give only a transiently blissful experience. But at the same time, it snatched many things, your happiness, your conversation, your information. In a moment you gained many things but then you could lose all, too. He meant to say that while he also used social media platforms like Tumblr, Facebook, Instagram, it was not correct as they were just 14. It was the lure of many things, like appreciation, love, etc. So, he uploaded pictures, got views and reviews and feedbacks, from his schoolmates. He even got an

award at a local competition for the best album that he had made. He created stories from his pictures. And all of these helped boost his confidence.
Then he asked her if she would like to answer the same question, to which she replied that she talked to very few people. These were people whom she liked, who kept their thoughts clear, and who didn't show hatred toward anything because they thought that all things had their own values. The people she generally loved were creative, who had a vision of their lives and who respected their parents. Anand smiled a little, then he asked, "Do you really love someone?"
At that moment, the bus had stopped for passengers to get freshened up during the night. Everyone was getting out of the bus, so they also got down. Once outside, Ruhani complained to her mother about feeling cold because of the cool winds. But her mother replied that because their bag was locked, she was finding it difficult to take it out. Hearing this, Anand said that he had a jacket, which he immediately brought out of the bus for her.
Anand said, "Ruhani, try it, I think, it would help you."

Ruhani looked at her mother for approval, and with a smiling face, her mother allowed her to take it.

Ruhani said, "Thank you, Anand."

They had dinner, and they ran towards an area from where they saw a waterfall was making a noise. The wind was cool and relaxing and the dimmed moon light was creating a beautiful moment. After few hours, they were going to take different transports for their different destinations, so they were simply drinking in that moment, together. They both felt that they were in nice company in their own respective trips. Sometimes we create big moments even in small trips or during less time.

Suddenly she asked him, "What do you think about this story, why don't you click pictures of these?"
Anand replied, "Hope I could, but sometimes few moments can't be captured, they are meant only to be felt."
When he answered this, Ruhani looked at him and smiled and he smiled back. After a few seconds, the time came when the engine started and the bus driver pressed the horn to alert passengers to get back to their respective seats. Everyone get inside, she asked his father for the mobile, for clicking picture. Then, he clicked his picture, and he gave that picture to Ruhani's mother. Before the bus moved, Ruhani ask for exchanging seats with the window opened. He agreed, and they continued talking about this and that. Finally, they fell silent. Now they were listening to their own thoughts. Ruhani was thinking about him, how a stranger becomes close enough with whom she could spend such beautiful moments. She was never going to forget these moments. On the other hand, Anand was thinking that perhaps he was beginning to like Ruhani. Even in this small meeting, when you met only for a few hours but you created a big story. As a teenager, he wanted to tell her that he needed Ruhani around him. But at the same time, he thought if she liked him it'd be great, but even if she didn't, he'd be okay.
While he was thinking all this, Ruhani slept off on his shoulder, and he kept looking out of the window. It was magical really, with none of the lights switched on except the cozy night bulbs that cast a dim blue shade.
The next day everyone got down, and started packing their bags and looking for their things lest they forget it in the bus. Anand and Ruhani also did the same, and when they were both finished with that, Ruhani looked at him, hugged him and kissed his cheek. Then Anand put his hand inside his bag and took something out of it. It was a box, which she opened after a gesture from him - inside that box was a flower clip that he had bought for her from a local stall. She thanked him. Everyone get outside the bus, said

bye to each other, and then suddenly Ruhani remembered his jacket, which she was wearing at that time. She thanked him for that for it had really kept her warm last night.

Now Anand and his family proceeded with their trip, they were to cover long distances, and Anand was filing his gallery with more stories inside the camera. Guwahati, then, crossing New Jalpaiguri, he remembered about her. They reached Darjeeling, the second place after Assam which was famous for tea farming. He met new people and was really enjoying every moment. Then they took a break and stayed in a hotel for some rest. There, Anand started checking his photographs. Then, he put his previous SD card, because in the middle of the journey he had changed it. While the pictures were rolling, he began to pick the ones he liked the most. He felt that he could write something about those. A few days down the line, his family reached Sikkim, and after 10 days they came back home. Then, he started changing the pictures on his walls. Few had stories, few had faces and few had feelings. The feeling of liking someone.

It's been 4 years, and I never met her again, but I am the one who was known for his photographic skills and I am in Canada for travel and a project. I don't know whether I should have confessed my feelings to her that day, that I liked her, or whether she already knew that. Maybe you remember I talked about my dreaming, and that I like to dream. But when a moment comes in your life when you feel you are in a dream then I don't think you should continue to dream - sometimes you have to start living on it. **I wrote a story about our meeting, and you are reading this, and it is obvious that I have done what I had said.** So yes, the one who is narrating this story was once a character in the story, in real life. Yes, I am Anand, and I hope she will also read it. By the way, at the beginning, I had told you that I want a female friend. I have several female friends, but now I need a girlfriend. You know what I mean. Keep smiling, keep creating your story, because every story is unique. Show some love to this book.

THINGS THAT NEVER CHANGE (MONEY, YOU AND TIME)

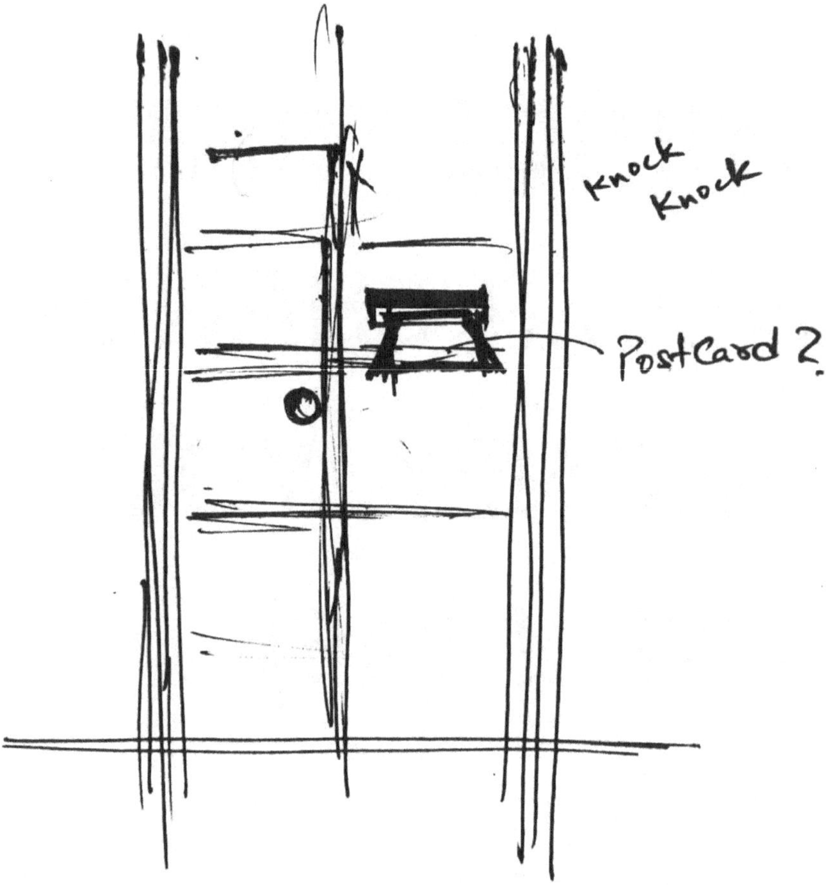

Hello, is somebody home? You got a postcard! Amazing fact, in the era of mobiles and WhatsApp, who is going to send her a postcard? She hadn't applied for a job, and she didn't know anyone who could send her a postcard. It was a big surprise for her. She signed the digital register of the delivery man. And then she took a bottle of water that was kept on the dining table. She satisfied first her thirst, then her curiosity - opening that postcard.

That postcard was from the neighboring city. She was searching for the name of the sender, but she what she found was a letter with 20 Indian rupees inside it. The first line the sender had written instructed her to buy whatever she wanted to using this money, click a picture of it and upload it in her Facebook newsfeed. A day after that she would get a mail in which there would be a surprise from their society.

Despite thinking a lot and conducting a bit of research she found nothing. To understand what was happening with her, she even called the police but even they didn't understand what this was really about. One of the policemen took it seriously so he told her to do what was written there.

So she went to the market, but without any idea about what to buy and what not to buy? For so many things could be bought from those 20 rupees. Panicking at her indecision, she asked a stall-person to give something which she could buy for those 20 Indian rupees. The stall-owner was equally confused, so he looked at the lady and gave her a chocolate worth 20 rupees. Not having a liking for that particular brand, she picked up another of her choice. Then she came back home, unwrapped it, clicked its photo and uploaded it in her Facebook profile. She got a few likes and comments, and she waited for tomorrow for the mysterious mail. The next day came, and she got a mail notification that she opened. As instructed in there, she went back to Facebook again. She found her feed was 25% filled with posts related to that chocolate of the same brand she had bought the previous day, and she kept thinking about it. Also, she found that many other had people uploaded pictures of other things like stationery, or other eatable things worth 20 Indian rupees. What was happening was really rather crazy.

Then another mail came, wherein it was written, 'Thank you for your effort and we want to know about your experience. What was your first thought about that postcard, and what was your experience regarding it?'

She replied to that mail, confessing that she had got confused after seeing the postcard, because that was such an old way of sending messages. After all, in the days of modernization and digitalization, she couldn't make out the use of the postcard. She also mentioned that getting 20 rupees was very confusing, too, as if someone wanted to gift her money why only twenty rupees. That day was spent entirely in confusion and many questions rose in her mind. She recalled how when she had gone to the stall her mind was not working about what to buy. Which is why she had taken the help of the seller for choosing something for her - and after that, she had exerted her own choice on it. Then when she had uploaded its picture on Facebook, she had got comments from a few acquaintances about experiences related to that.

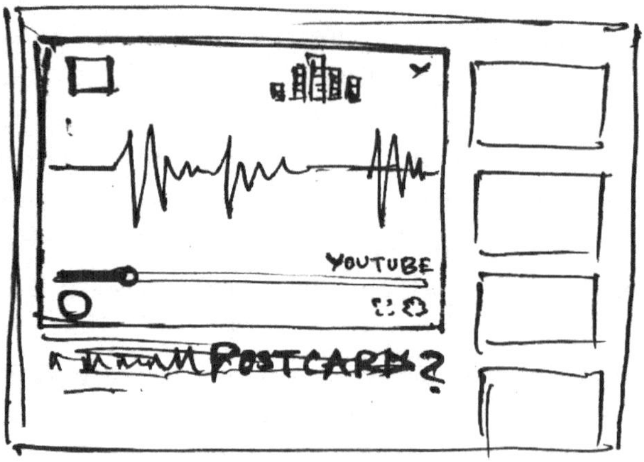

A mail came that said, 'Thank you for taking part in this craziness, you are now counted as one of those who are active, very nice.

This is just for society growth.' She was not sure what was happening, but it really stressed her. This whole part became a topic for several discussions, this thing created a harmless chaos to the extent that this was mentioned in the next day's newspaper. But nothing happened till 2 weeks. So, she also forgot everything that had happened to her.

After a week, a video started going viral. It was about the postcard. She clicked that video and saw that it showed an interview of a hacker in which he had explained everything about his work and other activities.

Interviewer – Who are you?

Hacker- I am unknown.

Interviewer – What did you do in this week?

Hacker- I threw a ball and watched the full game, without playing in a field.

Interviewer- Can you elaborate what's your motive?

Hacker- That's why I came here to get myself interviewed. For I want people to listen to me.

Hello every one, this is Unknown here, no one has the caliber to trace me. Besides, I haven't harmed anybody, no one was harmed, no one lost their money, no one got hurt. At least, I hope so, and if you are hurt, then sorry about that. I just want to convey a message to everyone. Because this is more important for those who were innocent. Two years back, I went bankrupt because of some reasons. I am not targeting the system, I am not targeting any field. As I said, I crashed financially because of few cheats around me. In my childhood, my father taught me how to use money and how to earn it. Then I wondered how I could save it for tomorrow. I used to save for buying things that I needed the most, but as I lose patience rather fast, and rather than buying useful things I bought useless things. And then I felt regret about it. I didn't enjoy what I bought. This is something that most individuals do. In these two years I read many things, I learnt many things.

So, I thought I had to share it with all of you.
First of all, I wanted all of you to listen to me, so I chose the medium of a postcard for it. Because in this society, if you are doing something unique, then questions are raised, otherwise no one notices it. I am going to show you how I manipulated everyone while sitting in this chair. Do you find anything suspicious in that postcard? I know the whole thing is suspicious for you. Yet, I want to ask this, what if somebody uses that? If you do not, then pick up that postcard, and check other postcards. Post cards have pin codes and addresses in them, and yet it was all faked-up. Only the post office address and street name is correct. Ha-ha, so yes, most of you find it real as it is, when you get to know about such things, many of you called the police. That's what I wanted, I needed attention, I needed people to think that something suspicious was going on. Oh, I know they also don't understand this, this whole issue was revolving in and around nothing. If you can stop there, nothing would go wrong with you. But if out of curiosity, you replied to that, well, a chain of events started. Many of us performed well, instead of your scheduled posts, or a regular work, you were engaged in this - with which you have no relation. So, I hacked your time. Then at the same time, Facebook was filled with posts with no faces, only and only brands and products, but still no one knew why they were doing that. That's what I want to show you, no matter how safe you are inside, anyone can hack your details, data, or anything without doing much.
Now listen carefully to what I am going to show you. First, accept the things that are connected to you - you are the only one responsible for your decisions related to them. Maintain your patience level. Before taking any action, read, learn, explore what is happening with you. And the most important thing, sometimes, our action speaks much more than our words, whether negative or positive. Being a constant is all you need with the wrong things. On social media platforms, many of you get unknown and

irrelevant messages as request, from which they need your engagement, which you accept or reject. When you reject that request, they get engagement, which is what they need. That means if you don't like that thing, ignore it, being a constant is all that you need to maintain in you.

My family was destroyed, my wealth gone, and I am the one who was hiding all this from you because I lost something. And if I gain something I will come up with a new identity. These things are going on with each one of us. We are always surrounded by people. Each individual loses something and meanwhile he/she gains something, too. So you have to be aware of where you are headed or what your actions were yesterday, not for others but for yourself keep yourself alert. At this moment you are ahead in time and digitally connected but if you want to be safe make sure you know what a postcard is? Because **these things never change: money, time and you**. Money will always be there, because we have utter need of it. Time you have, its free, but we own fear because sometimes we don't know what's happening with us. I know you have time, that's why you replied to my postcard. Make sure you don't save your time. Instead, spend it on what you need from your life. You see, you pay for life from your time.

Now coming to the topic of fear. Fear of the unknown is much bigger than any fear. We have never seen a ghost, but we talk about it, and sometimes we have believed it. We have stories, few with a background, few are fake. Someone makes an image of a ghost that looks terrifying. We create stories, we create plots, humans can do anything. So even if you didn't see how a ghost looks like you definitely have the fear of it. And now we are too ahead in time, but that thing becomes so strong, that someone watches it for entertainment, someone doesn't and someone continues to argue about its existence as to whether ghosts are mere tales or stark reality. Why am I talking about fear? That's because your fear is data for those who need you without your permission. That is switching to the third thing which never changes, and that is you. Now you may have questions that you have differences in you, that you speak differently, you became something, your work changed, your place of living changed. Moreover, you changed after hard times. For that I want to end this with some questions: What is your name? What are your likes and dislikes? What's your past? I know all are related with you.

(A few seconds went by but no sound came. There was complete silence on the other end)

Interviewer – Hello! Hello! Hello, Sir? Sir, Are you there?

THE LOVE NO ONE TALKS ABOUT

This story neither started from a bus stand nor from the conventional meeting in a café or wherever you can imagine the best place, like the mountains, the beaches, etc. I remember, a few years back, this was one of my most desperate dreams. I am not talking about the dreams that we see while sleeping, I am talking about the dream that we can see anytime, which we can feel and we can live on. The magical dream of sitting beside a nice person who kisses my cheek while saying, "You are my love." Did you experience the craziest love ever? If yes, then I am one of you and if no, then keep imagining my story, because this is not a story which is impossible for a regular person. This is what makes the world go round, after all! This is not the story you read in the fairy tales, this love story was created which revolves around you and your dream. This is the story about **the love that no one talks about**.

My best friend called me around 11pm. Like always, his first quote was, "I was busy that time that's why I didn't reply to your messages." I had heard this line many times from him, and as always, I asked him what exactly was he up to, and why he didn't get any time to talk. That became our weekly routine - having a conversation around the weekend without counting any hours. We keep our time aside and enjoy that moment.

One year ago, I called him, for I felt I needed to talk to him. Like always I found him discouraged, bowed down with problems in his life, hurt deeply. However, he smiled and pretended to be fine in front of others; even with me he tried to appear cheerful.

I got annoyed as I was his best friend, but he wasn't sharing anything with me, and I did not know why. Maybe there was a trust issue. Most of the time, I figured out his situations, but I was kind of a normal girl. How could I get to know his situation when he would not share it? I shared my happiness, problems even my thoughts, but he never did. Sometimes I got disturbed and wondered why he called me his best friend, for I think best friends are meant for sharing everything: happiness, truth, trust, sadness.

In a corner of my heart, I continued to like him. I always smiled when I saw him, I always teased him, and though I hid my smile from him I liked it when he was around me. Robin surely deserved a certificate of uniqueness, for he was a multi-talented person while still being a soft-hearted boy. Though he really is an idiot for me, and he'd always be one, for the whole of his life. I don't know what my connection is with him. Whether I liked him or loved him, I didn't know. But truth is, whenever I felt alone or something, I wanted him only. Maybe a few of you will identify with this situation but I have two best friends because I am lucky. Another best friend is my high school friend. I share many things with her, maybe much more compared to Robin. And she is the one who came first. Robin is in the second place.

I saw Robin at my coaching classes. He was skilled and serious about his career, and he was one of the people who were called less talkative. But in that class, there were more than 70 girls and 40 boys, and I found him to be strange. First of all, he was from another batch, a late comer, i.e., he had joined late. When two batches were combined for a class, he entered. I didn't notice him before, but as he was showing his confidence in front of others, answering the teacher's questions no matter what others will say, it grabbed my attention.

He was focused, many of us were just looking for cracking the exam to get a chance to enter college, but he was different. He came first for learning, then for competition, cooperation, friends and at last for the exams. Many girls were attracted to him; well, maybe not many, but definitely a few. Few called him for help for solving questions, few for hanging out, but rarely did he find time to be with others. He just came to the coaching class, did his job and went back home. Then I found him on social media. Many classmates already followed him; again, not many but a few were his friends there. In the classes, many guys try to flirt with girls, hang out with them and be the ones to make the first move. But I saw him rarely interact with others. He chose to sit in one of the first three rows and never looked back to check what was going on. After a month, he started interacting with other boys and girls. But no one could believe that he was such a talkative guy! How I came to know this? That's an amazing story by itself.

First let me introduce myself. This is Helena, the one who is narrating this story to you. Make sure you imagine the things I am mentioning. I am an introvert; I like to interact less with new people. But with the one who is close to me, I can talk to them for hours, any time. I found myself among a group of about 8-10 people. I was aiming for a better future. Sorry for lying, I want only the best future as in which I can own my own world. Other than that, I don't really have a focused aim. It doesn't mean I don't have vision, I have. I work, and I have dreams. But sometimes it all gets drained out when laziness comes about. I am a lazy type of girl. I hope you get a summarized character sketch of my personality.

Let's continue with the paused story. I searched for him on social media, I followed him, yes it was Instagram, for the Facebook days are gone. He had an amazing profile, which reflected his creative personality. I found him active there, despite doing all the assignments given in the coaching classes; he was one of those who were always prepared with it. I don't know how he managed all these, but yes, he did. Few days, we had a nice conversation, virtually. But when we came in front of each other, we didn't talk to each other. He also had a conversation with my one friend with whom I came to class. She asked him for taking the same public transport as us, and he agreed. That day we were waiting for him, and he joined us soon. We took our seats and our conversation began. That day we both friends got to know that Robin was the one and only who could talk so much without giving others a chance to speak! We found him to be talkative, which contradicted his facial expressions and actions in class. The one who was oh so serious and focused also had the quality of talking nonstop. That day we came to know that he lived alone, in a room, where he cooked for himself. He loved travelling, and he loved to talk to new people. If I were to introduce his skill of talking, then I would say, he is the one who can talk to anyone else without any hesitation. He talked as if he already knew the other person very well. After many days, we started spending time together. Sometimes he took me to a museum for showing me news things, on other occasions, to some equally informative place. Truly, I will say that while he was new to that city, he had come to know the city much better compared to me - one who was living there for years. He loved to explore things, he loved to travel, and he didn't need any vehicle. If he didn't find a mode of transport, he chose to walk, and he walked covering long distances of 6 to 8kms per day, depending on his mood. That directly showed he is energetic. And if I looked at myself, I preferably waited for a vehicle to come rather than walking like him. Sometimes I thought he was crazy.

As days passed, our connection grew stronger. Sometimes he made me happy, sometimes he made me angry. And this resulted in our strong friendship. For some reason, he left the coaching classes - joined late, but left earlier. I missed him terribly. When I wanted to meet him after the classes, sometimes I called him, and he'd join me. We spent hours together. Things were going smooth and easy for us to share with each other. The harder I thought it would be talking to him, the easier it was going on. Now he was getting so close that I could feel for that person. I liked that guy, though he was still a complicated person. But I don't know how I came this close to a person? I found him to be busy, but while he didn't have time, he still took out time for a meeting with me.

And then, a day came, when he was leaving the state. Day before yesterday, we met, we spent time together for hours, and then during a public transport ride, I kissed him on his cheek. I thought I was very close to that person. I liked that person. I never thought that how such new things could cause many changes in one's life. What all had happened with me after his entry in my life! He responded by kissing my cheek. I realized that day that he loved me too, though we were friends still. We went to our colleges, he was in another state, and I was in another state.

Now I missed him even worse. But now we spent time talking weekly.

Unfortunately, this did not continue for long. After a few months, something terrible happened. We fought badly during our mobile chat, and then we quit talking to each other. I liked that guy; sorry, I loved that guy so much. But we quit being together.

Months went off. These days were really going hard for me. Yes, I could see his updates in social media, he continued with his work, he continued with his life, he moved on with our friendship. I talked to my first best friend, Samantha about all this. She helped me to forget about him, she helped me to forget everything bad that had happened to me.

But one day, something crazy happened - I got a text from him asking about me. That day I didn't reply, though after a few days he again sent a message. To this, I replied and then he called me. We talked again for hours and then everything cleared out. He accepted his mistakes, and even I accepted mine, and after this, our connection got stronger.

Then he said he liked a girl, and he thought he loved her too! I was shocked, but I knew deep down this was going to be his infatuation. Still, like a true friend, I helped him to get her convinced. I saw him, excited for her, and while seeing him in bliss, I felt very satisfied. I just didn't want to destroy our friendship. So, for confirmation, I asked him if we could still be best friends. He agreed. The girl he liked, I began to see her actions from the eyes of Robin.

Doesn't it show Robin is not an idiot? I mean, yes, he is, but anyone can be diverted when he or she gets distracted. Yes, it's hard for me to accept that he won't accept me. And I cannot ask him about loving me, because I got my best friend back only recently and couldn't risk losing him again. So, I found myself in a better place by not going ahead with this strong relationship.

Two months ago, he called me. It was a Sunday, when we had our usual talks, fights, and teasing. All of a sudden, he proposed to me! I thought he was kidding like he had done many times. And he loved a girl already, so it was hard to accept what he was saying. I went totally silent.

Yes, the guy whom I loved had finally proposed to me. This took a long time to reach my head, I thought I was dreaming. But it was real, the person who generally got proposals from other girls, the person who rejected all of them, the guy who loved another girl as of now, was actually proposing to me! That was really so confusing, and I had many questions to ask. Then he replied with a note revealing that girl he supposedly loved was just a story he had created, just to know his place in my life. As I selflessly helped him, it created a big confusion between us mostly for him! He wondered what he had to do then, because the girl he was talking to, the girl who was his best friend and who was loved by him, that was I. He told me that he liked me years ago, but had the fear of losing our friendship. So, he didn't ask me out then. But that day, he proposed to me. He said he loved me, he added that I was all that he wanted, and with me he found a deep connection. But like other relationships, our relationship got too complicated. He still didn't share his situations and I had issues with myself. I am rather short-tempered and both our mistakes were destroying our best times together again. But this time, I was very happy that I had him for good. He knew how to manage my temper, he asked for forgiveness, and slowly he was sharing his hidden truths, too. The guy I knew was very soft, only he didn't see anyone with whom he could believe he could share himself with because many bad things had happened to him. He had got bullied at each and every place, treated as the most useless person and got separated from many of the people he held close to him, and he was not able to forget all that. All of this was hurting him deeply from inside. After that, and even today he finds it difficult to understand me properly. We fight most of the time, and in this Samantha helped us both. Yes, he also knew her, so he also talked to her. But if you don't want to go with self-realization, nothing will get good automatically. So, we started a conversation to help understand each other first. The guy I knew was not too bad in this - he was just tucked somewhere in the middle of his life. We shared, we talked about what we didn't like about each other, and what we liked. And clearing everything made our relationship even stronger. He was now showing his real face, the guy I love was rude, idiotic, harsh, complicated. Still on the other hand, he was loving, caring, creative, and romantic, a simple person.

This is what happened to us, and we think that every problem is with the other person. No, that's not true. If you really want to break up, there is something in you that you are hiding from that person. Put across all your things in front of that person, then ask him or her to put forth his or her every like and dislike. If there is truth from both sides, then there will the possibility of a strong relationship. We talk about being loyal to each other. Truly, it is a basic requirement, but have you really been loyal to that person? Don't blame him or her for your situation. If someone really wants to save a relationship then, he or she must definitely make it clear and better. Yes, the hard truth is that we think stuff like what if that person leaves me, or, he or she knows me very well, or that he or she is going to hurt me using my secrets and my weaknesses. And the answers for that start from questioning yourself. Do you understand that person very well? Do you really know him or her? Do they really have that special place inside you or are they just for casually talking and hanging out with. Because a relationship is all about being together during the good times and also during the bad and the hard times. Many of us hurt ourselves, telling ourselves that we took the wrong decision of getting into a relationship. But after everything, when the wrong decisions and their impacts are behind us, we get back down, we do the same again. It is not bad, but always blaming time or always blaming yourself is bad. Understand your feelings, understand the situation you are going through, and if you are feeling better at that time, it is good for you, because you are enjoying it. But don't blame others, or hurt others for the bad that may have happened to you. You know, each one of us knows how we frame sentences, truth, conditions, even our life. And we know how many people know our secrets and how many do not. If that person is good, then I give you my word that person will not use your weaknesses against you until you hurt them too hard.

Many relationships fail because of any of these things going wrong - either they don't know him or her properly, or maybe they can't handle the situation, or don't know how to balance things. Two factors that are always going to change with you **are time and age**. Why do many people say time plays an important role in a relationship? Well, they mean to say about having patience in bad situations and accepting new things that happened to you while you are in that relationship. Yes, in my case, if he wants to leave me, it's not going to be a big issue for me, because I am loyal to him, and I know so is he. No matter for how long it goes, we are going to enjoy this, because there are many things from which we always get unnecessarily disturbed. We can be sad for things, but if we can extract any happiness from anything, accept it. If someone said, you deserve better, if someone says we need to break up for XYZ reasons, okay fine, accept it. And if you want to clear the air then clear it, what he or she wants to say or what you want to convey to him or her. The more you look clean and clear, the stronger your relationship will be. And the stronger even you are going to be. Most of the time we cry because someone hurt us, but we don't understand how to move on... Yes, if you go in self-realization mode, you will get your answer. Because we are not perfect. We can learn to make things better, but it doesn't mean we become perfect.

"Ask yourself, why you love someone, and then stick to that statement for a long time after being loyal to that person."

Someone said that love is what you expect. Someone said, love is what you need, and someone else said love is something you feel. But I will say, love is what we pray for, it is what we have to keep faith in, and it is the deep connection between two persons. It doesn't have any rules to bind you, or for you to you follow blindly. This love is a product of natural, not artificial situations. Neither did I think what time was decided for me, nor did he know what I felt about him. But what we both know, and even you do, that love is what you can believe in. You just have to keep patience and wait for the right actions. There is energy, there are mutual feelings, there is truth, and there is everything. Even the **love that no one talks about**.

ONE DAY LATE; TRUCK DRIVER

"Where are you going?" asked Nangthoiba. It was one of the common names of a native Assamese. "I am going to fill water from that nearby waterfall" Liam replied. Liam was one of the best drivers in North-East India. He was known for his 15 years' experience and driving skills. He was from Manipur (one of the beautiful states of India, one among the seven sisters).

Till one day ago, these were two different persons who generally did not accompany each other while driving trucks. Nangthoiba had his own truck to drive but his father took it for another work to Shillong, Meghalaya. So, he was alone. Then there was Liam who didn't have any co-drivers for his truck. He asked Nangthoiba to join him.

Liam was very well-known among the truck driver communities. But few drivers were jealous of him just because he was down-to-earth, skilled and humble, and traders generally preferred him for loading his truck with their materials. So Nangthoiba agreed to his proposition and the contractor gave them a job with 2 big containers. Inside that was the material for interior work worth more than 50 lakh rupees. For the first time in their job history had Liam and even Nangthoiba got a job as big as this. And for this big loading, they were going to be paid more than they usually got. So while they were both excited, they were also very afraid of the terms and conditions set by the material owner.

The owner wanted that material in Guwahati in less than 12 hours because he had planned to load it on train for a long journey to Kerala. And they both knew that the travel time from Silchar to Guwahati was minimum 13 to 14 hours even without considering any time loss at road due to traffic jams, landslides, or any other emergency. So, it was really a challenge for them. Besides, one more thing was against them - it was the rainy season, the month of August. But they promised that they would try to reach as soon as possible.

The loading time was set, and they were asked to be present in Silchar at 4pm. Now the clock was tick-tocking to 12pm, and they

were getting prepared for the journey, bidding goodbye to their loved ones. Liam promised his son that he would get new clothes for his family after he came back. Meanwhile, Nangthoiba washed their truck, and both of them worshipped their vehicle, in the name of Lord Vishwakarma, the God of machines and engineers, worshiped by Hindus in India. They believed that worshipping their vehicles would ensure the safety of their lives and that of their vehicle, as even that is a part of their family. They moved towards the signboard, which was only half-visible (rubbed off because sign boards are not taken seriously in many places in India). Well, the SIGNBOARD read – straight to SILCHAR 20kms.
"Luck always finds a way to help you on the way, you just need some experience."

"This is going to be a new experience, Nangthoiba, and you are lucky for me, thank you," said Liam.

Nangthoiba replied, "As you are feeling lucky to have me as a companion, so after this deal, what about 1 quart of beer together?"

They both laughed together.

The containers were loaded on the truck, the truck drivers were also ready, and they filled up their fuel tank and proceeded on their way to Guwahati.

Maybe you have never heard of the Seven Sisters. Maybe you never got the experience. Maybe you just know the geographical aspects of North-East India. So here I am sharing a poem which will draw a few mind-maps of the Seven Sisters.

Seven sisters who never worried,
For whom they are getting ready,

They never need make up of design,
They are already known for their beauty.
Arunachal Pradesh in a deep green,
Even the Himalayan range bows to it.
That will never stop to Nagaland,
The beauty of untamed old human culture.
The water from Manipur and Mizoram,
Flowing down like the hairs of a girl.
Meghalaya has its own extraordinary skills,
But known for her waterfalls and mountains.
The state Tripura connects the valley and the mountains
Shaking hands with Assam.
The tea garden known to be its cloth
And she is surrounded by all her sisters.
People are of an enterprising nature,
Even girls are known,
For their power and education.
Here is the love, here is the beauty.

In the first few hours of travel, Nangthoiba was driving the truck on the National Highway that connects Sricona, Kathakaal, Panchgram, Badarpur, Karimganj then Kalain. These places are the initials where small towns and small cities were established. Their population was quite dense. Tall mountain ranges could be seen after Kalain. They parked their truck at a nearby petrol pump and checked their containers, the last time before driving ahead, given that high-altitude driving was to start They were to drive up to the mountains utilizing too much engine power and had to make sure about the security of the material as well. It was now 10pm, after 3hours of driving, and Nangthoiba parked the truck at a Dhaba for having dinner. They both had their dinner and bought a packet of cigarettes for killing sleep late in the night. Now Liam took over the steering wheel because rain had started falling heavily. They started again to cover the long distances, talking about this and that. Liam shared how he was once scolded by his wife because he came late at night and how she worried for him so much if he stayed in wet clothes for a few hours. To this Nangthoiba added, “I don’t have anything to share about my wife, for I am not even married, but my mother scolds me often if I go hungry during my drives.” Then Liam said, “This is really not good, Nangthoiba. Regular food intake is good for us, for us drivers can only eat two times per day. You also know spending days and months on roads is quite tough. Yes, now it’s a habit but just like soldiers, we don’t get to meet our families for long time periods. By the way, meeting family members, specially the loved ones after a long time, I really enjoy that moment.”

Nangthoiba agreed to his statement after sucking the cigarette smoke and nodded yes.

"Distances, this is what the full story is about. We meet people; we experience roads. We take deals, we take challenges. Everyone living on this earth is living with at least one challenge. Maybe it is about living life, or getting famous, or buying food and clothes. Or maybe it is about one change..."

They were both rather enjoying their ride. After covering a distance of 100kms they reached a place called the death zone of vehicles because during rainy days, the height of the mountains made them look like a giant with a widely open mouth. Due to landslides, many roads break down such that only one vehicle moves at a time. And that creates a traffic jam more than 5 or even 15-20kms long. But the drivers of buses, travel SUVs, travel vans, and trucks are very experienced in that. They can move their vehicles very cautiously and with alertness. In fact, bus drivers are sometimes so kind that they don't even care about their lives - they drop the passengers first and then cross that precarious part of the road without caring about themselves. And if they slip or there is any lack of alertness on their parts, they are just swallowed by that MOUTH OF DEATH. Oh, it's too deep, nearly 200m or maybe more.

After that death zone, they crossed two more, and they knew that they would be late because of these.

Now they knew that they had to reach very fast because it was already 2am. After a few hours they reached Ladrimbai (a corner of the Meghalaya-State). The roads of that mountain range were very notorious for their accidental zones. Now Liam asked Nangthoiba to take the steering. So, they swapped places and Liam rested a bit. Now the steering wheel was in the hands of Nangthoiba. We know that Nangthoiba was known for his speed and 30-degree speed turning and overtakes. So, within 1 hour they were both inside a deep forest amid high mountains.

, having covered a decent bit of their distance.

Current day, 5am morning.
"Where have we reached, Nangthoiba? Why are we not moving?" Liam asked.
"Just 2-hours away from Shillong" Nangthoiba replied.
"WHAT!!!!" Liam shouted. "But why?"
"There is a big jam, people were saying it stretched for 10kms ahead..
"We have to reach before 9am and we have not even reached Shillong. So, what do we do now?" Liam was too disappointed with this situation.
Now that both of them knew about this situation they talked to the owner. But he was unrelenting and wanted his goods early. That's why he had promised to pay more.

That region was known for low mobile network places. Only the deep forest and the people who were travelling on the mountains could be seen in abundance.

Nothing to eat, even not a hope to move. The road was looking like a snake which crawled for a few minutes and then stopped.

Now the morning was too beautiful, in the view of the new people, but not so for the drivers. After 4-5 hours they had seen many native tribal female and children, with fruits and few fried seeds on their back. Passengers on the jam-stuck buses, especially women and children who were too hungry were buying those. This showed the clear difference between the two groups. One was travelling, with access to many common consumer goods. But in these mountains, these native tribal groups couldn't get anything - just a happy face that was worshiping the name of nature.

That view of nature was very hard to dislike, but the rain drops blurred the glass. It was the wipers that helped show clear view of it. The sun was on the top, and its rays made ways to enter to deep forest after the dark rain clouds. THE RAYS WERE LIGHTING UP THE RAIN DROPS ON THE LEAVES AND THAT SHOWED A BEAUTIFUL VIEW OF STARS OF THE DAY. Still the situation could never be called normal, full of struggles as it was.

Many people went to nearby waterfalls from where they took water for cooking rice or whatever else they had. As drivers experienced such situations so frequently, they were used to taking stove and cooking materials with them. Like many others, Liam, too, took out his stove and kept it by the side of the truck. Nangthoiba set a plastic sheet as a roof above it for saving it from the rain. Someone was cooking rice while someone else was engaged with dal or any other edible stuff they had with them. After a few minutes, Liam began to walk away.

"Where are you going?" asked Nangthoiba.

"I am going to fetch water from a nearby waterfall. We will boil it and use it for drinking." Liam replied.

Liam came back after getting cool, fresh and natural water. Then Nangthoiba went there, washed his face, and sat atop a big rock near the waterfall. Its waters were falling down with a loud gush. After a few hours, they heard a voice, "EVERYONE GET READY! THE JAM IS GOING TO OPEN UP." Everyone who had been troubled and worried by this jam, the passengers and truck-bus drivers like Liam and Nangthoiba who needed to be in Guwahati at a given time, immediately felt relaxed after hearing this. Everyone started getting ready. Few finished a last smoke, few folded their tents set between the trucks and few drivers woke up hastily from under the truck where they were catching up on their sleep.

It was now 8pm and it was too late. The rain was coming down thick and fast, matching their heavy mood. Suddenly, a sound echoed between the mountains and the deep forests. It was the sound of many engines revving up at a time. The dark was suddenly lit up with the glare of hundreds of headlights turned on at once. The **Snake of Traffic Jam** started glowing for more than 10kms. It was almost as bright as daylight. Now the snake was moving, slowly. But lo! Moving for a mere few minutes, it stopped! Thankfully, after a pause, it started moving again. This is how it was moving now, stopping and starting at intervals. Liam and Nangthoiba were praying fervently to god for their payment because they had already lost their hope of reaching Guwahati on time. While they were discussing this, they reached the bottleneck area which had caused the jam in the first place. There was a big rock that had broken off from the mountain and fallen across the road. Its pieces (one of them equal in size to one 6-tired vehicle or truck) were scattered all over. Some pieces had damaged the road along the side. Even the bridge had been broken into two parts. Soldiers of the Indian Army and many civil workers had reached there from Shillong and were engaged in the essential repair work, because this place was close to that accident zone. They saw that the workers had built a temporary bridge and only one big vehicle was passing at a time. When it was their turn to cross that bridge, they were both highly nervous, worried that the bridge was shaking in the wind. And when they peered closely for a few seconds they could make out two trucks and one bus that had fallen down in the abyss below.

Well, they passed that bridge safely. The rest of the road was clear. They could drive at top speed. Both were fresh and wide awake. Liam was driving, and soon they reached Shillong, where they skipped their dinner despite having decided to stop there earlier. They had now planned not to stop till they reached Guwahati.

Nangthoiba took the steering wheel now and drove across many tiny hamlets and villages. The naturally cool wind hit their glasses as they overtook the trucks, even the speeding ones, but the eyes of both the drivers were filled with hope. No matter how challenging was the heavy rain, their truck would never stop before they reached their destination. Suddenly Nangthoiba's mobile rang. Liam answered the call. The caller asked, "Where are you? You know that this deal is critical for each one of us. So reach there immediately." That was their Contractor who had given that deal to them. But before they could reply to him, the network was lost and the line went dead. They were now in even more fear of losing their payment.

All of a sudden, Liam's mobile started ringing. The caller said, "Can you tell me where you are stuck, and are you both fine? I just heard that two trucks and a bus were swallowed by death." It was the owner's voice.

"Yes sir, we are safe. We are moving at a high speed to reach Guwahati as soon as possible. And thank you for your concern," replied Liam.

Suddenly, Nangthoiba yelled over the roar of the engine and traffic noises, "SIR! WE WILL DROP YOUR MATERIAL WITH FULL SECURITY, DON'T WORRY. JUST MAKE OUR PAYMENT. WE HAVE HOPES FROM YOU."

The owner replied "You have time, you can drop the containers till tomorrow morning 8am. But make sure you won't delay beyond this time because you are already **one day late, Mr. truck driver**."

"Sir my name is Nangthoiba, ha-ha..." Nangthoiba replied with a laughing voice. They were relieved now, though they couldn't believe their luck. Maybe any time soon a new problem would arrive. Nangthoiba had lessened his truck's speed during the call to ensure they got the perfect network, and about as soon as the call ended, they heard the unmistakable blast of one middle tire puncturing. The truck had to be pulled over to the side. Now, it takes 1 and half hour to repair a truck's tire and re-fix it. Thankfully, it was 1 am and they were just 3 hours away from Guwahati. With the tire fixed, Nangthoiba handed the steering wheel to Liam. It was time now to display Liam's driving skills. He lit his cigarette and finished smoking one cigarette over more than 60 kms. The road from Shillong to Guwahati is well known for its well-maintained status, as also the curves, the C-curve, the V-curve, the dangerous one, and the loop-curve. They both were enjoying the turnings, and who will not, after hearing this great news that they were going to get paid.

When we looked back at their travel, they appreciated the struggles they faced, risked losing their precious wealth, and even their lives. Maybe they would get no payments at the end, because they were late and they had just had a close encounter with death. But seriously, I can see the hope, I can see the kindness, I can see the concern. Yes, they are lucky enough that they are getting their payments. Many others didn't get these chances. Life always gives a chance to correct your wrong decision, but what if you never did anything wrong and you don't even get the chance to correct? Yes, the main reason was time, business, and the under-privileged classes/groups of the people.

Yes, they reached on time, talking to the winds. They were paid a little extra because they hadn't even stopped to eat something.

Liam said, "Nangthoiba, I think I am going to be scolded by my wife for not eating food during these driving hours just like you," and they both laughed, enjoying their drinks. That day they read the headlines, how from the collision of the two trucks had caused 3 drivers to die; one was in the hospital. While the passengers of the bus were safe, so were the two drivers. They read this headline silently, because perhaps they could be in their place. They congratulated each other and went back home. Liam took his family to buy new clothes and Nangthoiba bought a new sari for his mother on her birthday, to which Liam was invited, too.

"You never know when your big chance will come. And you never know who you are, what your skills are, unless you deal with the tough situations."

And I think you need to visit North East India because the roadways are now much better than the old times, and there are many train lines which run on the mountains. But one thing I will tell you - if you never get **ONE DAY LATE**, you never experience the other side.

WHEN IT'S ABOUT A GIRL

(Reading)
"Sorry, this is too late. I think this letter will reach you after days of delay. As I was very busy these days. Wait, let me hold this, did you take your medicine, are you even continuing or did you stop it....

"Alice, first give me that medicine otherwise my love will start scolding me. You can then continue reading that letter," said the male, middle-aged patient.

Alice smilingly nodded her head in agreement with his words.
She gave him biscuits to eat, then gave the medicine with water.

"Do you want to eat something else, "Mr. Perfect?" Alice said.

"No, not now, because I want to hear Daisy's voice. After that I will take my meal. You now take that letter and read," he said. He lifted his brows in the direction of the letter, which was kept on the table.

Alice continued to read.

".... I know you stopped it, and now you will take that medicine. Wow! What a great habit, Mr. Perfect. Do you want me to stop writing you letters? If yes then tell me..."

"No!" he shouted, he cried and said, "I don't want you to stop writing letters, I just wait for your letters, MY LOVE."

Seeing his condition, Alice tried to hide her tears.

".... If you don't want me to, then for the third time I am asking you for the promise that you will eat all the three meals a day, take medicines on time, take proper rest and most importantly, be happy. Yes, I know, for a few days I am away from you, but don't you think that during this time we need a strong understanding with each other? I don't think I have much to tell you but I know you want to keep hearing from me, right?

"Mr. Perfect, do you remember you loved to play table tennis, and how you made me win, breaking all rules? You know, I don't have anyone with whom I could play. When I come back, I want you to get ready for another defeat because I am learning to play this game and have hired a trainer for me. I will defeat you while following all the rules, keep in mind. And moreover, I must mention that my days are too busy now-a-days. Last night, I forgot to eat my meal because I had to complete my work. Now don't get tensed about me, I take care of myself much better than you do, darling idiot, my Mr. Perfect.

"And I think I have to give up calling you Mr. Perfect and start calling you Mr. Idiot. What do you say to that? May I? OK, so, take care. I will wait for your reply. You start getting ready for that game. Keep working, keep running, keep enjoying.

Your Love
Daisy

All of a sudden, he asked, “Why does she write so less?”

“Maybe because she already told earlier she was quite busy with her official works,” Alice replied.

After a few seconds’ gap, she said, “May I ask you why she calls you Mr. Perfect? Because I always see you lying on this bed. Is this what she refers to? You are perfect at lying on the bed the whole day!”

“No, No,” he laughed. “That’s not true, Alice,” he said. “Let me tell you. I think you remember her first letter, in which she talked about me, how I care about my work, my surroundings, and others and it leads to my work getting done perfectly. *That* is why she addresses me so. But tell me, I can’t remember how I got here. One day I slept and when I woke up, I found myself here.”

“Say, don’t you want to eat your meal now?” Alice asked, sounding evasive.

He spent a few minutes thinking about the letter she had just read out and said, “Okay, take me to the dining room.”

Alice said lightly, “You are Mr. Perfect, but can you prove this to me?”

“Ha-Ha, okay, let me try.” He put out his left leg first, then maintaining his balance, he put forth his right leg and then tried to stand.

Alice quickly took his hand and put it round her shoulder for support and said, “Hey! You really took the challenge! I am really happy to see you standing.”

So they had their afternoon meal and then he demanded that Alice help him go inside his garage.

This garage had its own story, and Alice wanted to know that very much. So they both navigated down to the living room. That room had a side door that led to the garage. His eyes were showing his excitement as he had risen from his bed after a long period of time. With his fingers he felt the objects he had made or modified. All of a sudden, he pressed a book with his fingers, and it turned out to be a switch to a secret door. As it opened, Alice was shocked because she didn't know about this hidden door.

"Mr. Perfect, what is this?" she asked.
"This is my secret workshop. Do you want to see it?" he replied with a smile.
There was a staircase that led down, taking which they reached down to a platform. All of a sudden, the darkness turned into light. Alice was again astonished, and wondered what this was.
She moved about and saw a beautiful sculpture of a couple, which was covered in a thin film of dust. "What is this?" she asked.
"This is my eighth wooden craft, which I have made for my love", he answered.

That wooden craft showed a girl and a boy dancing together.

Let's take a short break in this story and light up the character sketch of this man. His name is Leon Carter. Mostly, he was known by the epithet Designer Carter. He owned three big companies. Before this traumatic situation, he himself used to run these three companies, or rather say navigate the direction of success for these companies (CRAFT COMPANY, HARDWARE COMPANY, and CAR MANUFACTURING AND DESIGNING COMPANY). He was known for his craft work, ideas, mental ability, hard work, his teachings and leadership skills. He generally spent his time in his garage where he did many things. And on top of all this, he was also a state champion in Table Tennis. People around him respected him enormously. He had lost his parents in an accident when he was still a child, but he never went back to his past looking for sympathy. He worked hard, focusing on developing his skills. Sadly, his other family members left him alone, thinking of him as a burden. Instead of lending a helping hand, they falsely blamed him for stealing food, material and even money. But if you are the boss, then even time bends down on its knees. So, about time we got an insight into Carter's past. What now, then? Now he was inside his secret room with Alice.

“Don't touch it! Otherwise it will react with your hands!” Carter shouted. But by then this bottle had cracked and the liquid had come out.

"That was a chemical that reacts very fast with human skin. Take this tool to pick the broken glass," said Carter. Alice used that tool to pick it up and threw it in a dustbin. She then moved forward to a wall full of photographs.

She saw several photographs of Carter receiving trophies for his many inventions, and work leadership skills. When she is slightly got focus to one corner of photographs, there she saw a few men laughing, clearly in mockery, at Carter as he stood with something broken. Then in the next photograph she saw those people were holding him on their shoulders and enjoying his victory. How much a man can change? Being bullied by people is healthy for us to encourage us? No one, be a girl or a boy, is helpless if they take their own identity seriously. We always are the ones who were hungry for anything, which is good but why do we want to prove or need to prove our worth to those harsh people.

We are strong. A child is strong when he is born and fights so many diseases to live in this new world after leaving behind the shield of the womb. A teenager is strong when he or she starts working on his or her aim or target without any distractions. A man or woman is strong when they are successful in fulfilling their needs and take care of three stages of life that is the 3-stage family. If we hold this here, two questions arose at the same time - one is, are we waiting for that situation and second is, are we hungry for that situation?

"Being alone is a situation decided by time. What if you decide to change it?" asked Carter.

Alice suddenly turned back and saw Carter coming closer to her, taking careful tiny steps. "These are the photographs which I never want to show to anyone else", continued Carter.

"Why so, Mr. Perfect?" asked Alice.

"With time, I have learnt many things. If you want to, then I will surely teach you."

"Yes, I want to learn." Alice said eagerly.

"So, TIME always says, if you will follow me then you have to follow my rules. What I want to show you, what I am going to offer - everything I do should be accepted by you. But if you walk "with me" I will give opportunities, I will give advice. But you will get your right to choose the right or wrong. Even if you choose wrong, I will still be with you to give you a hand and pull you back on your feet.

"As I don't want to show these photographs to you just because every time, I see myself as a backward person until I overcome my fear of losing. This nature, people, society, system are all my teachers but yes, I always try not to blindly support or follow everything. I analyze, choose and think just because few people will accept you because a few people love you, a majority need you and few don't really want to.

Carter took a stick which was on the desk and pointed to a photograph.

The photograph showed a child holding a plant in his hand with a note written across the flower pot.-

"If you are growing a plant, give them the proper amount of water and sunlight. Sometimes it lacks essential elements of growth due to weather change. But if you know how to grow then even if it stops growing for a while it will become green again, even after the so-called death. Everything you lose or win, it will live for 100 wins." Carter smiled

That day was spent with a smile on Carter's face. Wait, Alice also felt relaxed that day.

THE NEXT DAY

The doctor came, did his check up and said, "He is getting better. Take care of him, he will be fine soon, those days are near."

That last day, Alice wanted him to play table tennis but Carter showed her something which she had never ever thought about.

Naturally, Alice needed to know more. So, after giving lunch and his medicines to him, she went down in search of something more. This was her opportunity; Alice went inside and searched about this man. Because she wanted something more from him. Now the days were passing and Alice had started with her research on the house.

What was she looking for? No one knew.

'So, Mr. Perfect is rich. That's an advantage,' said Alice to herself while searching for something inside a box. 'He is unaware of his own identity. Can I use it for my advantage?'

As she was engaged in searching the box, she found something that contradicted the image of Carter that she had in her mind.
First of all, his full name was Leon Andre Carter. He was known as Andre during his teenage. He lived in Europe, but moved first to Canada and then India when he came here for tourism. He mostly roamed in places like the Northern- Belt states and then the North- Eastern Region. Then one of his company partners cheated on him and got him fired illegally. To hide this, Carter changed his name, cutting out the Andre and becoming Leon Carter legally. Then he began to grow his business through his sheer struggle, skills and hard work. That was the reason when his achievements grew bigger he never took it for granted, for he just loved his work, he believed in growing. He didn't stop exploring and experiencing India - temples to bamboo houses, lakes to rivers, heights to flat lands.
The box had many hidden stories inside. As Alice continued searching, she thought that this box was something like magic. The deeper she went, higher the chances she found something. She picked up an envelope about 12 years old, sent in February. It was a letter from a place in India called Tripura. The photographs showed many memories and interesting facts related to India and mostly the North-East India.
That letter said,
"Hello Sir, we are organizing the function of Bamboo Art and Culture, and you are invited along with few other artists. All arrangements will be done by our team. You have to join us for five consecutive days.
With regards
Organizing Team"
Alice put her hand inside the box again and found 20 pictures of that function. All those pictures were of a girl. She was Daisy, Carter's late wife.
Just like those envelopes there were many more and Alice searched for all of them, read ALL OF them during these four days,

which went away in a flow. Clearly, now Alice had much secret knowledge regarding Mr. Leon Carter.

One day, all of a sudden, Carter declared he wanted to play table tennis as now he had almost recovered. Alice agreed to this. Thus, they started spending their time playing table tennis. In fact, they both started enjoying eating, roaming, playing, and talking together. Alice was now feeling very heartened as she noticed Mr. Perfect's improving health. It took Alice just a few weeks to learn to play table tennis. Serve-Shot! Block-Hold! SMASH! Just then, Carter remembered his wife Daisy who hadn't written to him since two months now.

"Alice, do you remember we didn't reply to your ma'am, my love, Daisy? We need to write her a letter. Let's go," he said.
He took out his favourite pen worth USD 200. With his improving health, he thought that instead of narrating the letter to Alice, he would write it himself.

"Hello Dear,
I am ok now. In fact, I am better. Alice, she took such good care of me. Sometimes even better than you. Just kidding! Just come fast, so we can lunch together, as she also lives in my house. So, when are you coming back? Do you remember that secret chamber in the garage? I visited there after such a long time, but everything is fine there, in its proper place.
You remember the first ring that I gifted you? But why is it not on your finger? Did you keep it there?
Okay fine, we will talk about that later. By the way, I want to inform you that I am going to start my work very soon. Hope you are fine. Have your meals on time and don't take too much stress about work. And yes, come back fast, because I am going to defeat you this time.
Your love

Andre"

Significantly, that letter was taken by Alice and posted to the address. The next day, Carter decided to analyze the business aspects of his company and get back to work. He went to his office and called his office caretaker and the old team of workers who were still employed by him. Alice was with him, and she had already talked to the senior management for work-related arrangements before Carter had decided to re-join his work field. She settled everything and instructed everyone not to ask Carter about his health or anything else. Everyone agreed to discuss only works-related topics. Everything started once again in a proper way, now that the right skills were in the right place. Carter was back and all faces had got their smile back.

Days were going on, the three companies restarted with their big deals and profit-making. As Alice had planned, she became the manager of two companies given by Mr. Carter. She started her studies and three days a week she gave time to those companies. She learnt many things from him, and now she was even liked by many of the workers because of her kind behavior and work strategy.

"Who said girls can't do anything or they can't do a man's work? They can, just give them a chance."

But in this story, what did she decide for her? Maybe we can know in the next page. Now Mr. Carter had completely recovered. One month passed, two more months passed, and Mr. Carter started working at his office.

One day, he went to his store room in search of a file. There he found a stack of old newspapers. In every newspaper, there was a news item that reported a train accident. All of a sudden, he remembered his past. While he was experiencing all this, he suffered from a severe bout of headache. Alice got this message about his condition from one of the employees working there, and she immediately returned to the company office. There she called the five people who had been closest to Carter.

The caretaker held Mr. Carter and gave him a glass of water. Suddenly, a voice echoed.

STOP NOW! CONTROL YOUR EMOTIONS, MR. PERFECT.

Carter knew this voice, it was similar to the one he had heard many times addressing him as Mr. Perfect. He looked up and saw Alice was standing in front of the door. There was pin-drop silence in the whole office.

"How do you know me?" Mr. Carter asked.

"I am a girl whom you took care of right from the day I came to this world, DAD!" Alice said.

"Daughter! Alice?" Carter suddenly started crying.

"Yes, she is your daughter, and I hope you will remember her perfectly." This was spoken by a man standing next to her, holding her hand.

"Ibrahim? You? I thought you had left my company, and that you had left me?" said Carter, bewildered.
"Maybe I did, but your daughter always kept us united," said Ibrahim and the other four people nodded their heads.
Both Carter and his daughter Alice hugged each other tightly and her shoulder was soon wet with her father's tears.

"Your mom, left us, she died." Carter said.

"I know, but I know this also that I have a hero to always take care of myself. It's you, my father. And I need you with me." Alice replied.

"Yes, Andre. You have to forget the past and take care of her," said one of his oldest friends.

His crying face was transformed into a smiling one because he was with five of his closest friends and his daughter.

One of the five friends said, "May we talk at your home?"

The office was closed and everyone went to his home, the bungalow. They called the doctor for the last checkup.

"What happened to me?" Carter asked.

"After the train accident, Daisy died on the spot and you were taken to a hospital. You suffered traumatic amnesia and forgot the past. The one thing you remembered was your relation with your beloved wife Daisy. And this was affecting your daughter the most."

Carter felt too guilty as a father. Then he looked at his daughter, who stood looking outside the glass of the window.

“Sorry, my child”, Carter said. “I don’t know what happened to me. I was just stuck there.” Alice turned around and hugged her father.

“From the age of 12, she wanted her father to hug her but he never did. So she just she took a pledge to cure you first,” said Carter’s friend Robin, who was standing next to her.

“What did you expect from her? People think parents are responsible for bringing up their children. But your situation was such that Alice had no parent in her growing up years. She taught herself the manners and values that she has today. I am proud of you, Alice,” Robin said.
“So, Carter, when you were in bed for eight to ten months, she took care of your every need”, Robin informed.

“Wait, but I got letters from Daisy.” Carter said. “My child, you know this, tell them.” Carter continued, gazing at Alice and prompting her to speak out.

“Dad, that was me,” she replied.
“WHAT?” Carter was shocked.
“Yes Dad, I wrote all the letters and there are more,” Alice said.
Alice had more than 10 letters in her hand. “Every time you wanted me to read out instead of reading the letters yourself, you helped me out unknowingly. May be few things will not be seen in these letters because those few lines, I framed while reading out to you. In this your best friend Mr. Millington helped me a lot. He gave me enough information about mom and your relationship and I highlighted them in these letters.”
Time went on slowly, as the moon went just above the roof and everyone left them alone. Now just Alice and Carter were left.
“Dad! I want to show something,” Alice said.

"Yes, sure my child," Carter replied.

She took him to that secret chamber and told him that she gathered the rest of the information from there. They talked late into that night about every photo which was taped to the wall. And at 4 o'clock in the morning Alice asked, "What about the Table Tennis match?" And she laughed.

"It's now morning and today is Saturday, so let's play one match", Carter said.

They played three consecutive matches and shockingly, his daughter won 2. The last match was won by Mr. Carter, after which he picked up his daughter and started shouting, "I won the match and I got my trophy." Yes, the trophy was none other than his daughter.

POETRY SECTION

The poems are written based on the experience and the imagination of the author. The poems have their own character sketch

This section reflects an interesting part of the author's life. In this section, he has introduced many things, and showed how he experienced those things in his life. Every word, every line is inter-related. He wants to show the effect of time with words. Sometimes poems without rhythm increase boredom. For this, he has tried to help you with their inherent meaning. Read the full poem and then you will get to know how it relates to your life and how it has its own beauty and tune inside.

It is the author's expectation from readers to feel the poetic figures - whatever he has mentioned in each line in each poem. According to him, everyone has a tune inside, make sure you know it.

THE PHOTO ALBUM

I am 75 years old now
Yesterday I lived my whole life
One day I took birth
And everyone cried
Today my glasses are
Awash with drops

Second day I crawled
And everyone clapped when I walked
Now I have a stick of royalty
But no one clapped

Third day I have a book

And I slept off
Head down on the desk
Now I sleep but no one scolds
And I don’t even get the best dreams

Fourth day is my favorite
I loved a girl and
We had to break, for the other had charm
Now I have my wife with me
She is my fifth day memory

Fifth day I kissed a girl
College dipped into study and enjoyment
Now I am old
And still she kisses my hand before sleep

Sixth day of my life
I worked and became the root of a tree
Now that tree was
Graced with branches, leaves and fruits

Seventh day I cried
I have a second life
A fist holding my finger once
Now I need his hand to stand still
When first he said ‘huu’ when he speaks
Now I have to say ‘huu’ for call, I am leaving

AUTHOR's PEN (THE PHOTO ALBUM)

This poem was written based on the experience of a man who is already old, and after a long time, he is experiencing his whole life. He captured the cherished moments of his life and pasted them in an album. This album is the reflection of his life. In this poem, every page is meant to be a day, an important chapter of his life. Forget for some time about the digital gallery, and remember your album. Where did you reach and how has it changed your life? It will be a great experience, seeing that album rather than your gallery. Do you have any album? I hope you have your own stories inside.

MY FESTIVE CALENDER

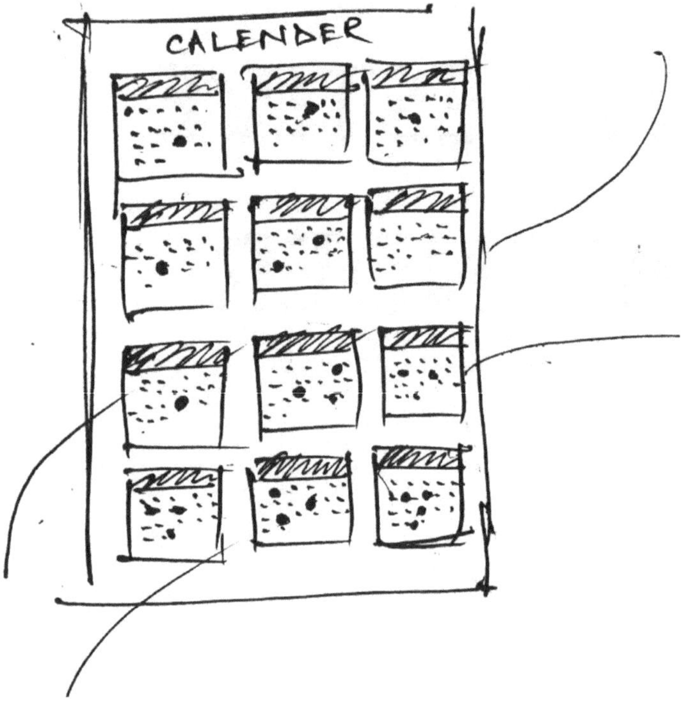

I planned my holidays
The Sundays were included
But it was an excitement always
On the calendars, holidays were highlighted

It was really bad
When holidays picked up Sundays
But when they're joined with it
Then enjoyment increased in fun-days

Indian festivals left their remark
When Muslims called others to join Ramzan
And everyone visited Gurudwara with a smiling arc

Hindus shared fruits and Christians asked for Christmas eve

Colors of March went off, then April presented sweet dishes
It went on turning the pages of the calendar
When Hindus invited for dinners and lunches
Then love increased when December ended with decoration

We tick, we fill, encircle the numbers
We pictograph pre-planned places
There is always a change of seasonal differences
But still we enjoy the days called holidays

AUTHOR's PEN (MY FESTIVE CALENDAR)

While thinking and reading about the Indian culture as I went back to my old days, remembering my childhood, how I planned my holidays. Sometimes those days went crazy, sometimes plans got cancelled because of the seasonal changes. But we waited for holidays in schools, always thinking what we were going to do, and inviting others for joining us during festivals. I don't know, but when I was a child, I never heard about what humanity is? And what we have to do for maintaining it? Because in schools we already knew our friends' names first and then his or her religion. And about that calendar that hung on my walls, sometimes it was plain, sometimes it had many pen markings over it.

Word box

Smiling arc – smiling face

THE MAIL BOX

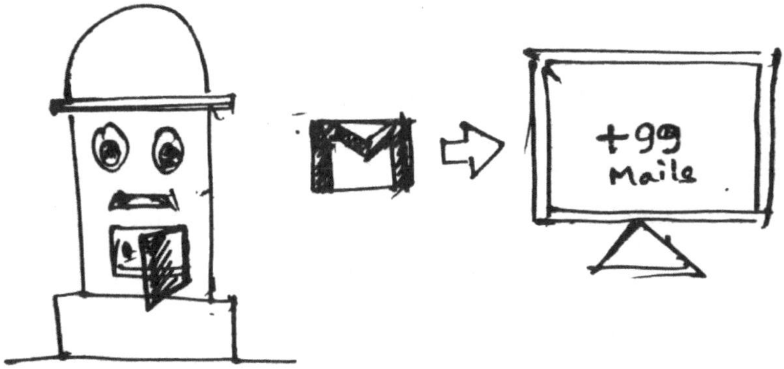

There is the truth of a red box
It had moments inside
In the streets, it kept
Hundreds of emotions

The past went off
It lasted before, how valuable it was
It has its dress, but now it's old
The stomach was empty and it can't hold

It was THE LETTER BOX
We now have digital mail
The paper, now its screen with no loss
Called it is not a fail

There is no failure
There is no loss
Save trees and save nature
Creates a new chaos

Here and there mails are sent
"Trees still cut down in search of space"
Who will save the nature?
Everyone hands up, we are in a race

Mails are running, found the work done
Still mail box was filled, but there are no emotions
There is no one whom you met as messenger
There is a filled mail box, without any motion

AUTHOR's PEN (THE MAIL BOX)

Did you see an old LETTER BOX by the streets? What do you feel about it? I know you are thinking that it is outdated now. Is it really? Do they lose their importance? Why they are not being painted since years? Just because we have e-mails in our e-mail boxes. The poet tried to recover its value through his poem. Once he was just roaming in the streets without any reason, and he saw a letter box that looked like an old man standing and looking at the streets. How it develops, and he is the one who sees all the changes. Yes, time plies ahead, we never look behind, but the poet wants to remember that LETTER BOX. Once it housed his letters filled with emotions. Did you send a letter to someone special?

YES, I LOVE YOU

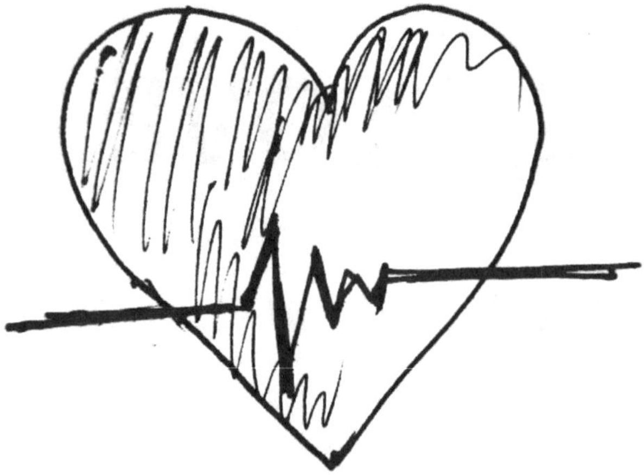

I clear my anger
Every time I wrote
The text bar shows me
Options of loved short notes

It was hard to cut you off in the middle
Dominance of my soul whistled
It's bowing to you, looking at your shoe
I just want to love you

People name it as a weakness
And I am saying it's my kindness
The harder I am, the ruder I look
Over-possessiveness is not me, which I ever took.

I remember I hold your words

And fantasize over them in my dreams
We are above the mountains
And holding all seasonal-rings

If you are away, I am holding my time
If you are close, I am holding you
The day when you ask do you love me?
From the day I felt, still I am saying, yes, I love you

AUTHOR's PEN (YES, I LOVE YOU)

This poem is clear. We all know how this phase comes in our life, when we love someone. Together we spend time. If we are far, we make lists of things to do together, dreaming about them and fantasizing about them. Few days are not normal, and we don't want to hurt anyone, still at the same time we get angry at each other. Before being called a writer, I was just a poet of romanticism. In those days, people used to ask me what is love? I know many of you have your own answer to it, but what I know is a simple answer to this question: love is which I can express to her, love is what makes me feel what my responsibility will add on. It is what teaches me to be grounded. It is what gives me my first freedom above my boundaries. It is what creates a new world, one which I have to manage with my love, balancing our needs, desire, feelings, time and mostly us.

Word box

Seasonal ring – different seasons in a year

I HAVE

KNOTS

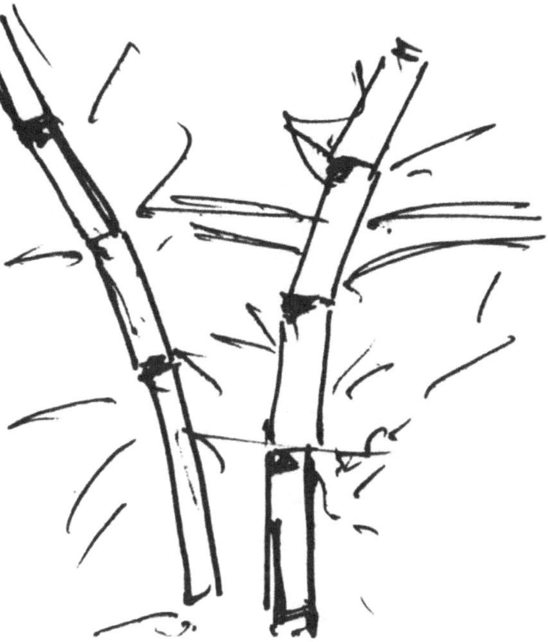

My growth is fast
Mother Nature feeds me at birth
I grow in forests
Forests where my body
Used as a support
I was white someday
And I changed to green
But I turned brown when I lost my feet
When I am young, I stand still
I'll bow to earth when I will be old

I was torn and used as a container
The first pipeline came to know
Northeast India utilized me

I was the lifeline for people
The rice was cooked inside me
The strong houses are of me
From the start of tree-house
To the multi-storey building
I was making up to great designs
From the fencing of the house
To the small pots I was known

Yes, I was designed, I was used,
Everywhere and in everything
I was the first bridge in mountains
Roof to walls, table and chair
The flower basket to utensils
Yes, my name is Bamboo
I am the well-known plant
Used as pieces or as a whole
Everyone respects me for the body
And hope you know I am a part of nature

AUTHOR's PEN (I HAVE KNOTS)
This poem is written based on the experience of living in the North East Region of India, The Seven Sisters. It has its own beauty that is too difficult to bind within words and lines. Bamboo is a critically important part of nature here, which is known for its beauty, uses, growth and importance to the natural habitat. This poem can help you gain some information about how they are used, how they grow, and how their beauty is. Wait a minute, did you visit North-East India?

Word box

Lost my feet – when the bamboo was cut down

I HAVE GLASSES, AM I LUCKY?

I can see far, I can see clearly
But there is something wrong
I can move but I can't react
To the surroundings and the yellow light

Yellow, yellow, it's a deep energy
The land below my feet was hot
There is the shade of my umbrella, but
The path was crowded and wet with rain of tears

My left has noises, even the right side
There I saw my old pages of regrets
They were pinned to the ground for remembering
This is what my time decided

Oh! That's my past, when I never succeeded
This is the truth, I am against my growth

The pages were old and torn
But the written dates and lines are still the truth
Maybe I've to lose my umbrella
And get used to that rainBlaming the surrounding was not enough
Otherwise your tears will be counted

A thunderstorm of rudeness was ahead of me
The day I started, it was always facing me
The dark frowns of the society
And I am facing the fog of time

I was glassed, and tired of motivation
But still I can't see far due to this fog
One step ahead and a new story
Another step, a new one, or everything will repeat

AUTHOR's PEN (I HAVE GLASSES, AM I LUCKY?)

This is the poem which I wrote when I thought I was all alone in this society. Quite easy to say that this society will harm you, and our parents became an umbrella to protect us from the rain of negativity, but somehow they became weak facing the thunderstorms of society's harsh truth. The way I am going ahead is new, but I have to deal with it. You have regrets, you are weak, but the world you are living in will stop you, will kick you back. Yes, but it will also make you strong. You have eyes, its better, but if you wear a pair of glasses you still are a normal person, because those glasses can help you to see clearly according to your eyes, not the society. Did you feel this is your story?

A PAIR OF SHOES

It's deep, when I walk on
The stones inside daze my movements
A pair of shoes is the mirror
Still the soles look the same

I remember my childish shoes
It was a palm-sized fancy
It never gets dirty but it gets loose
When I make 5 and 6 moves

My dear feet, you are growing
Maturity is standing at the door
The day, size shows the reality
When first you were hurt

Shoes are the reason

But why were they torn?
They reflect the hard times
When you first walk on

Here that was the child
My feet were touched to maturity
Still there is no one crying
When the feet were red

Shoes were new someday
They are appreciated for beauty,
After a hard time, they were replaced
And the feet appreciated for the struggle

AUTHOR's PEN (A PAIR OF SHOES)

I know you have remembered everything, for even you love to choose a new pair of shoes. Yes, you could have understood this poem very clearly. Rather than explaining what I wrote, I am going to tell you why I wrote it. This poem was written when I was seeing my album and I looked at my shoes. That's how this poem grew. I began to think how these shoes could be related to our lives. This really rejuvenated me as I thought instead of giving credit to life why not tell about life with respect to our shoes.

THE NAME

Yes, I have a name
It is an identical image
The name still doesn't have a pen
Which creates a picture of my age?

There is a prism of identities
And we are living in an illusion
Where everyone is unknown to me
I am known to everyone.

I am not THE NAME
Which can create my expressions
Just a NAME holds my fame
The definition by people's assumptions...

Create a thought about me

You will have a clear picture
Can you NAME it?
Yes, you can, until it's proved wrong

Yes, I am what you know
The small ant, or the elephant
But if you put me among humans
I am THE NAME

AUTHOR's PEN (THE NAME)

This is the poem which you may not have understood because this poem didn't reveal what I wanted to say. But if you pick the words one by one and relate it with that stanza, things may become clearer. For example- in the first stanza, I wrote identical image - that shows my name, your name or anybody's name is independent of its identity. My name doesn't prove what my character is, does it? The name came first and then we built our character. So, if you are looking for my age and want to compare it to my name and character, then make sure you know this. I am THE NAME. The NAME whatever you want to pick for me, but I am THE N-A-M-E.

To Publish Your Book with BookSquirrel Publication

Contact on-

Mail: info.bsquirrel@gmail.com

Instagram/Facebook/Twitter: @booksquirrel__

Website: www.booksquirrelpublication.com